W.i.t.c.h.

Will · Irma · Taranee · Cornelia · Hay Lin

The Disappearance

Adapted by **ELIZABETH LENHARD**

HarperCollins *Children's Books*

HEATHERFIELD

THOSE WHO HAVE ALREADY TRAVELLED HERE KNOW THAT, AS ITS NAME SUGGESTS, THIS TOWN WAS ONCE FAMOUS FOR ITS FIELDS OF HEATHER....

WOOOSH

BUT HERE, HEATHER IS NO LONGER FOUND. IN ITS PLACE ARE ONLY WEEDS....

...AND SILENCE.

NO ONE THERE?

LET'S FACE IT....

...ELYON'S GONE.

BUT SHE DIDN'T JUST VANISH INTO THIN AIR! PEOPLE DON'T DISAPPEAR JUST LIKE THAT!

I THINK WE'LL SEE HER AGAIN....

HOW CAN YOU BE SO SURE?

I CAN FEEL IT, TARANEE! IT'S SORT OF A HUNCH....

...AFTER ALL, ARE WE OR ARE WE NOT GUARDIANS OF THE VEIL?

RIGHT...

WHAT...WHAT ARE YOU DOING?

DON'T WORRY...

...JUST IN CASE SHE DECIDES TO COME BACK TOMORROW!

WHAT ON EARTH DO YOU THINK YOU'RE DOING? SOMEONE COULD HAVE SEEN YOU!

IT JUST SO HAPPENS THAT NO ONE IS AROUND!

BUT SOMEONE COULD HAVE BEEN!

BUT NO ONE IS!

BROM

BRR-BROOOoo

UH-OH... LOOKS LIKE ANOTHER STORM IS COMING OUR WAY....

ANOTHER ONE...

...AND THIS TIME IT'S A BIG ONE! LET'S GO!

SINCE SHE DISCOVERED HER POWERS, CORNELIA HAS GOTTEN EDGIER AND EDGIER....

I STILL CAN'T BELIEVE IT, HAY LIN....

...THIS IS ALL REALLY HAPPENING TO US!

IT ALL BEGAN A MONTH AGO. . . .

. . . AND . . . AND IN THE END THE TWO MONSTERS VANISHED! IT WAS INCREDIBLE!

BUT ELYON DID THE MOST INCREDIBLE THING OF ALL!

SHE LED US STRAIGHT INTO A **TRAP!** THE "DATE" IN THE GYM WAS FOR US!

I SPOKE WITH CEDRIC, THAT GUY FROM THE BOOKSTORE. . . .

HE SAID THAT HE HASN'T HAD ANY NEWS FROM ELYON SINCE THE PARTY, HE HASN'T SEEN HER OR HEARD FROM HER. . . .

SO SHE MADE IT ALL UP! BUT **WHY?**

WE'LL ASK HER AS SOON AS SHE GETS BACK TO SCHOOL!

SHE HASN'T SHOWN UP FOR THREE DAYS, AND NO ONE ANSWERS AT HER HOUSE!

WHAT'S GOING ON, WILL?

DON'T ASK ME. . . .

. . . THE ANSWER IS **HERE!**

"WE ALL WANT TO UNDERSTAND. . . . BUT IT WILL TAKE TIME."

HOW ABOUT A SNACK AT MY HOUSE?

OKAY!

THANKS, BUT I REALLY CAN'T. . . .

SEE YOU LATER!

BYE!

SEE YOU TOMORROW!

WHERE'S HAY LIN RUNNING OFF TO?

HOME! HER GRANDMOTHER ISN'T FEELING WELL, AND SHE'S WORRIED ABOUT HER. . . .

BRROOOOM

ONE

Will and her friends arrived at her apartment building just as black clouds in the sky began to roll, rumble, and spark.

As she, Cornelia, Irma, and Taranee climbed the stairs that led to the apartment she shared with her mother, Will glanced at her friends. It was hard to believe she'd known them only a few days! She already felt so familiar with Cornelia's long, blonde hair, Irma's smirk, and Taranee's raggedy fingernails. Will even knew that Taranee always gnawed on her nails when she was nervous.

In fact, Will thought, I bet I could practically read their thoughts. As she opened the door to the hallway and ushered her friends through it, she gazed at Cornelia's pale,

1

heart-shaped face. Her pink-glossed lips were pulled into a tight, tense line. Her blue eyes were steely. And she had the same expression Will got when she and her mum were having an argument.

Yup, Will thought. That's exactly how I look when I know that I'm wrong and my mum's right, but I'm not gonna admit it! And Cornelia's being just that stubborn about this whole magical powers thing. I mean, she made a vine come to life in the school courtyard. It slithered up her arm like a snake! That was magic! There's no other explanation for it. But Cornelia still refuses to say the M word.

As the girls turned a corner in the hallway, Will's eyes fell on Taranee, whose ever-clicking beaded braids were hidden under the earflaps of her big, floppy, red rain hat. Behind her little, round specs, Taranee's brown eyes were big and watery. Her chin was trembling ever so slightly.

She's wishing she was home, Will thought sympathetically. Taranee liked being tucked away in the safety of her photography darkroom or curled up in front of the fireplace.

And Irma, Will concluded as she gazed at

her, is wondering what kind of cookies I'm going to serve for our after-school snack.

As Will and her friends reached the loft door, she dug around in her pink backpack. Then she pulled out the big tangle of keys attached to the tiny rubber frog that was her key chain.

"Okay," she said, glancing at Cornelia's impatient frown, "don't laugh, you guys, but every time I try to unlock my front door, I seem to use the wrong key."

"Well, that *is* a lot of keys." Irma giggled, pointing at the crowded key chain. "Is this a home or a jail?"

"Good question," Will muttered as she fumbled through all the keys. The truth was, Will *didn't* feel as though the loft were her home – yet. She and her mum had moved to this seaside city called Heatherfield right before Halloween. They'd come here from Fadden Hills – where Will was born and raised.

Mostly, the move had been a good thing. Will had met her new friends almost immediately. And her mum seemed much happier now that she was farther away from Will's dad.

Come to think of it, Will mused with a frown, the only reason my key chain is crowded is that I can't seem to bring myself to take my old Fadden Hills house keys off it.

Will wondered what her new friends would think if they knew that she was clinging to her old keys, and her old life. They might think she was a total baby. Or that she was a little nuts.

Or, Will thought, glancing over her shoulder at Taranee's scared eyes, they might . . . understand. After all, even before we found out we had been given magical powers, we were totally bonding. Now, we share that major secret. And as everyone knows, secret-sharing is the first step towards becoming best friends.

The realisation made Will's heavy heart lift – a little. So her next thought was more of a resolution.

Okay, she told herself as she chose one of the shiny brass keys. If this key is the right one, I vow to take all my old Fadden Hills keys off this frog. Even the key to my old locker at the pool.

Will held the key up to the doorknob and bit her lip. Then she stuck the key into the lock. It fit!

And it turned! The front door swung open easily.

Will took a deep breath and thought, home, sweet home? Well, maybe . . .

Then she smiled and stepped inside. The girls crowded in behind her.

"Hello?" Taranee called out. Her voice echoed off the loft's high ceiling. Even though the apartment was lined with tall, multipaned windows, the place was dark and shadowy. The storm outside had turned the sky almost black.

"Come on in," Will said, glancing at her watch. Her mum rarely got home from her big, swanky office at Simultech early. "No one's here. My mother will be back in about an hour."

Will manoeuvred around a few cardboard boxes to hit the light switch. Naturally, she stubbed her toe on one of her own boxes filled with CDs.

"*Grrrr,*" Will mumbled, hopping up and down on one foot. Okay, she had to admit it. Another thing that might make her feel more at home in this new apartment would be finally unpacking all her stuff!

At least her friends didn't seem to mind the disheveled decor. As Cornelia unfurled the orange shawl she'd tied around her shoulders and Taranee pulled off her hat, Irma flopped back onto the comfy red couch.

"Man, I'm beat!" she said with a big sigh. "I wonder what's on TV."

Will stared at Irma for a moment. Okay, she thought, now I don't know if Irma's attitude is funny or scary. I mean, we're dealing with some heavy stuff here. She pulled off her beat-up, grey jacket and stood in front of Irma.

"You know," she began hesitantly, "with all we're going through, I'm not surprised you're tired. But aren't we taking this all a bit too lightly?"

As Irma opened one lazy, blue eye to gaze at her quizzically, Will went on.

"I mean . . ." she said, "we should be terrified. We have magical powers. Don't you realise that?"

Irma's response got an angry glare from Cornelia. But Will had to continue. "We suddenly find ourselves in the middle of something incredible, and we act like it is the most normal thing in the world," she said. "The other day we battled monsters, one of our friends has completely vanished . . . and we're here to have a nice cup of hot chocolate." Will tossed her jacket onto a chair and all but shouted, "For heaven's sake. How do you guys explain all this?"

"Hey," Irma said, propping her red shoes up on the coffee table. "Maybe we've got a few screws loose, and we never realised it before."

"Speak for yourself, Irma," Cornelia snapped. She folded her long, skinny arms over her chest.

Will threw up her hands and stomped back across the living room to the open kitchen at the far end of the loft. Taranee followed her and slouched in front of one of the tall windows.

Will grabbed the coffeepot and stuck it beneath the kitchen faucet. "There's something much bigger behind all this. I still don't really get *what*, but there is."

"As soon as Hay Lin's grandma gets better," Taranee offered, "we'll go ask her a few questions."

Will nodded. And at the same time, she cringed. The mention of Hay Lin's grandmother took her right back to that fateful moment just a few days ago. The girls had gathered – this time, for tea – in Hay Lin's apartment above her family's Chinese restaurant. The girls had been munching almond cookies and discussing their weirdly similar dreams when Hay Lin's grandmother had stolen in and dropped a bombshell on them.

She had smiled gleefully at Will, Irma, Taranee, Cornelia, and Hay Lin (whose names happened to form the acronym W.i.t.c.h.). And then she had announced that they were Guardians of the Veil.

And what was the Veil? Well, it was a barrier that had been raised eons ago between earth and the dark world of Metamoor. It was the only thing keeping who-knew-what sorts of gruesome evildoers away from the girls' own peaceful world.

Hay Lin's grandmother had explained that when the millennium hit, the Veil had grown weak. Creatures from Metamoor were then able to travel through it, by way of portals – which were sort of cosmic doorways.

To protect the Veil, some all-knowing spirit who lived in a place called Candracar had anointed Will and her friends as its Guardians. It was now their job to make sure no bad guys breached the portals. As the Veil's protectors, four of the girls had been infused with different powers – those of earth, fire, water, and air.

And then there's me, Will thought – I'm the keeper of the Heart of Candracar.

Within Will now was a small, orb-shaped, brightly glowing medallion. And it, apparently, was the key to the four other powers.

I felt this power in the gym the other night, Will thought with a shudder. Their friend Elyon had lured Will, Hay Lin, and Irma to their school's gym. She'd told them she had a date with a cute boy she'd met, named Cedric. But when the trio had arrived, Elyon and Cedric were nowhere to be seen. In their place had been a grotesque, reptilian villain and his monstrous blue henchman, a brute named Vathek. They were just the Metamoor baddies that Hay Lin's grandmother had warned them about. They were powerful. And huge. And dangerous. In fact, the snake-man had ordered Vathek to throw the three girls into a gaping hole. That's when the Heart of Candracar had appeared in Will's hand. Somehow – instinctively – she'd channeled its power. They'd gotten amazing, beautiful outfits, changed bodies, and even sprouted wings! Not to mention the power to kick the bad guys' butts. Which they'd promptly done. Unfortunately, their fight had also started a roaring fire in the gym. The girls had skulked away while firefighters arrived to save the building. And their secret identities had been discovered by no one.

That night had been only a temporary victory. Will knew other battles awaited them. What kind of battles, or with whom, was a mystery.

And that's why she and her friends were here, trying to figure out a solution to all of this.

As if she had read Will's mind, Taranee spoke up again.

"Until we know more," she said to the group, "we'd better watch our steps and keep our eyes peeled."

Will was about to agree when a tremendous thunderclap made her jump!

Sputttter.

"There go the lights," Will said, as every lamp in the loft flickered out. She rolled her eyes.

Could this day be any creepier? she thought.

Across the room, on the couch, Irma quipped, "I'd keep my eyes peeled, but I wouldn't see anything anyway!"

A Cornelia-shaped shadow near the couch said, "The lights have gone out, Einstein."

"Don't move," Will said, feeling her way around the living room. "Somewhere around here, there should be some candles or a flash-light."

"Don't bother, Will," said Taranee's voice behind her. "I'll take care of it."

And suddenly, Will detected a bright glow dancing through the air. She spun around in time to see a tiny, orange fireball, bouncing playfully in Taranee's palm!

"Yeow!" Irma yelped in alarm.

Cornelia gaped.

And Will gulped!

But she noticed that – for perhaps the first time that afternoon – Taranee's quivery, fearful expression had melted into an easy smile.

Taranee held her hand up over her head. The fireball tipped out of her palm as gently as a soap bubble and hovered in the air a few feet above Taranee's head.

Taranee nodded and grinned. Then she held out her hand again. With a muffled *whoosh*, another fireball formed. Taranee set that one free, too.

Before the girls could catch their breath, Taranee's sizzly spheres were bobbing all around the loft, filling the space with cosy firelight. When one of the fireballs drifted by Irma's nose, she reached for it with hesitant fingers. She gasped as one fingertip pierced the fireball, then emerged unscathed.

"Wow," Irma breathed. "It doesn't burn!"

Will laughed out loud.

This magic stuff isn't *all* scary, she had to admit to herself.

With a gleam in her eye, Will walked back into the kitchen.

"Okay," she announced. "Now it's my turn to show you guys something. Anybody want a snack?"

That question got Irma off the couch. She followed Will into the kitchen with a hungry look in her eyes. Taranee and Cornelia trailed after her.

"Yeah, I do," Irma said. "Have you learned some new recipes?"

Will leaned with false casualness against the refrigerator door and said, "What can we offer my friends, James?"

"James?" Irma cried. She glanced behind

her, then peered around the rest of the kitchen. "You have a butler and you never told us?"

Suddenly, a haughty British voice rang out through the kitchen.

"There's a rather meager selection, Miss Will," the voice sniffed. "Unless someone would be so kind as to restock me."

Will watched as Irma screamed and stared at the refrigerator, particularly the ice-dispensing lever in the freezer door. Without having to look, Will knew the lever was waggling to the rhythm of James's voice. Because James, of course, was–

"The refrigerator!" Irma screeched, pointing at the ice dispenser. "The refrigerator is talking!"

As Will dissolved into a fit of giggles, James continued.

"Ahem," he said, with all the dignity a refrigerator could muster. "I should bring to your attention the fact that the cream cheese next to the pickles has long since expired."

"Sorry, James," Will said. She quickly opened the refrigerator door and whisked away the block of cream cheese. It was, indeed, green and fuzzy. Then she turned to Taranee, who was back to looking trembly and terrified, and whispered, "James has very refined tastes, you see."

"The refrigerator is talking!" Irma shrieked again.

Cornelia stared at the appliance, then blinked.

"Bizarre," she whispered.

"The refrigerator is talking!" Irma yelled once more, this time grabbing Cornelia by the shoulders and shaking her.

"All right, already," Cornelia snapped back. "I'm not deaf!"

That seemed to calm Irma down. In fact, once she was through wigging, a huge grin formed on her face.

Will grinned back. After she'd gotten used to it, she'd come to adore her talking appliances. It was, perhaps, the only aspect of this new identity that *wasn't* terrifying.

"I discovered it the other day," Will explained to her friends as they headed back into the living room. "I can talk with all the electrical appliances! I've given them each a name and they do what I tell them to. They even work without electricity."

"Now that's what I call cost-efficient!" Irma exclaimed. She went back into the living area and flopped onto the couch again. Then she turned toward the TV. "Put on channel twelve. *Boy Comet* is on. It's the hottest TV show of all time!"

Will squatted in front of the TV. It was a rickety old set that her mum refused to replace with some sleek, new, flat-screen one.

"This one works fine," Mum had said, the one time Will had begged her to update their primitive set. Of course, now that her TV could talk, Will wouldn't dream of getting rid of it. Even if it was a bit crotchety.

"*Boy Comet*, Billy?" she said to the television delicately.

"Oh, no, Will," the wheezy old television rasped. "You know I just can't stand the musical theme song of *Boy Comet*."

"B-but, but," Irma stuttered. But Billy cut her off.

"My poor speakers can't handle it!" he complained. "Whatever happened to the golden days of easy-listening music?

"Now, what do you say to a nice documentary?" Billy continued. His screen sputtered to life. A big, fat bear could be seen waddling through a field of evergreens. Some drab flute music droned in the background. "For example, this one on *Globe World* about the secret life of black bears."

Irma gasped and glared at Will indignantly.

"What can you do?" Will said with a shrug. "It's a pretty old model. . . ."

Irma grunted in frustration and stared sullenly at the black bear on Billy's screen. The entire scene was so ridiculous Will couldn't contain her giggles.

"Every day, there's something new," she snorted. "Isn't it great?"

"Just great," Irma muttered.

Irma didn't turn Billy off. In fact, *she* seemed to get sucked in to the documentary as the narrator purred, "In the winter months, the social life of larger plantigrade animals reaches decidedly low levels. . . ."

"Uh, Will?"

Will turned to see Taranee pulling a computer disk out of her cloth backpack. "Since you've found a loophole in this no-electricity thing, could I print out my science paper?"

"Sure, Taranee," Will said, grabbing the disk from her bud. "I'll handle it."

Tailed by a couple of bobbling fireballs, Taranee followed Will into her bedroom. It was just as littered with unpacked boxes as the rest of the loft. But at least Will's orange laptop and printer were all set up. That had been one of the first things she'd taken care of when she'd moved in. Will felt lost if she wasn't wired to the Web.

And, of course, now that her computer and printer had come to life, they were more entertaining than ever. Will approached her laptop and braced herself for a little griping.

"Wake up, George," she said to her computer cheerily. "There's work to be done!"

"Work, work," the computer sputtered. His voice was high-pitched and whiny, with a definite northeastern drawl. "Nothing but work. I have a right to take a break, too!"

"Aw, zip it, George!"

"*Eeep!*" Taranee squeaked in shock as the printer next to the computer started talking, too. This voice was growly and low, but decidedly female.

"If there's anyone here who has to do the

dirty work, it's me," said the printer, whom Will had named Martha.

"Is that *so*?" George retorted.

"*So* so," Martha taunted.

Taranee gaped at the bickering hardware and whispered to Will, "They're fighting?"

Will shot her friend a wry smile.

"I think they're husband and wife," she said. "I could listen to them for hours!"

And now that I'm a Guardian, she thought, with a little flutter in her stomach, I guess I'll be able to!

TWO

Taranee joined Cornelia at Will's kitchen table. Cornelia had finished pouring some drinks. She'd also pulled out a jar of cookies.

Taranee sat down and nibbled on a cookie. As she chewed, she added three spoonfuls of sugar to her cup, and she kept her eyes cast downward. Part of her wanted to block out those fireballs she'd just conjured up. She also wished she could forget that the printer in Will's bedroom wasn't running on electricity – but on *magic*.

It's all just too weird! Taranee thought. It's . . . it's not right. I mean, yeah, making those fireballs was, well, *really* cool. But having that kind of power also kind of terrifies me.

Taranee sighed and thought about her

brother, Peter. Peter was a basketball hotshot and a surfer. Foul shots or ten-foot waves – Peter faced them all with his easygoing, surfer-dude chuckle. He was afraid of nothing.

Maybe I should ask him for some pointers, Taranee thought.

Or, she realised, I guess I could just ask Irma or Cornelia.

She glanced up at Cornelia. Her blonde eyebrows were knit into a stubborn frown. Irma was still flopped on the couch, dully staring at the nature show and taking loud slurps from her mug.

Taranee knew she could really only confide in one of her friends – Will.

Will probably knows just how I feel, Taranee mused. I mean, she's also a newbie at our school, the Sheffield Institution . . . I mean, Institute. She arrived just a couple of days after I did. I'm sure she wouldn't laugh if I told her that – fireballs aside – I'm petrified of this new magical gig. I mean, who am I to save the entire world from the forces of evil? I'm just worried about passing my history test next week!

Taranee was so busy brooding she didn't notice that she'd drained her mug. That is, until

Will's voice pierced her thoughts.

"Another cup?" Will asked. When Taranee looked up, Will was standing over her.

"No thanks, Will," Taranee replied with a sigh. Cornelia didn't even bother to answer. For a moment, the only sound in the room came from the little flickers and sizzles of Taranee's floating fireballs and the droning of Irma's TV show: "And it is in the summertime that the most reprobate of the black bears are at their worst."

Finally, Cornelia broke the gloom.

"So what do you think Candracar is?" she burst out. "I mean, what do you think this place 'in the middle of infinity' is like?"

That was how Hay Lin's grandmother had described it.

"You got me," Taranee answered. "But I'm more worried thinking about the dangers we'll have to face. What is out there beyond the Veil?"

"And who," Will said, sitting down at the table with them, "were those monsters we fought?"

The three girls paused for a moment. Frustration hung in the air between them until Cornelia spoke up.

"What do you say we do a little training over the next few days?" she proposed. She took a small sip from her mug. "Sure, we have powers, but we still don't know how to use them."

"Cornelia is right," Will said. She glanced up as the sound of tires skidding through rain filled the loft. As she got to her feet to peek out the window, she added, "It would be terrible if we created some disaster just because we were inexperienced!"

"Speaking of which," Irma said, finally turning away from her bear documentary, "I wanted to tell you guys something–"

"Oh, no!" Will interrupted. She was looking through the rain-spattered window. Now she was staring in horror.

All three friends crowded behind Will.

"What's going on?" Taranee squeaked. She felt fear send little prickles down the back of her neck. "What did you see?"

"Reptile-man and the blue gorilla from the gym?" Irma asked, moving in closer behind Taranee.

"Even worse, you guys," Will groaned. "My mum's home!"

With that, Will spun around. She pointed at the dozen or so fireballs bobbing around the loft.

"The fire spheres, Taranee!" she ordered. "Hurry!"

"Right away!" Taranee quavered. Irma was flapping at the fireballs with a *TV Guide*, but the flames did not diminish. She shot Taranee a desperate look.

"*Do* something!" she hissed.

Taranee took a deep breath. She knew the fireballs were her thing. But the problem was she didn't really know how to extinguish them. In fact, she wasn't sure exactly how she'd created them! She'd just sort of closed her eyes and dreamed of dancing flames. Suddenly she had felt a burst of warmth in her palm and – ta-da!

Now that she was put on the spot, Taranee felt paralysed.

"Oh," she whispered, wringing her hands anxiously. "What to do, what to do?"

She glanced at Will, who was running through the living room like a banshee.

"Television, off!" Will ordered the TV, with a flick of her wrist. The screen immediately went black. Then she ran towards the bedroom.

Taranee took another deep breath.

Okay, she thought. Clearly, I have to learn to talk the talk. She squeezed her eyes shut and opened her mouth.

"Fire, out!" she said loudly.

When Taranee opened her eyes, she . . . could see. This was *not* a good thing. The flaming spheres were still dancing around the room!

"Out!" Taranee shouted again. She pointed at one of the fireballs in irritation. "Come on . . . extinguish! Go out! *Poof!*"

But the spheres continued to flame. Now, their playful bobbing seemed willful and taunting. Cornelia and Irma stared at Taranee in alarm.

"Hurry!" Cornelia hissed.

Almost sobbing with anxiety, Taranee finally stomped up to one of the fireballs. And before she knew exactly what she was doing, she found herself pursing her lips. She planted her face right in front of the flame and blew.

Sssszzzzzz.

The fireball disappeared, leaving nothing but a wisp of smoke.

"Cool!" Taranee breathed. Then she began

to run through the kitchen and living room, snuffing out every sphere in sight. Finally, there were just the fireballs in Will's bedroom to contend with. When Taranee ran into the room, Will was pleading with Martha.

"Printer, off!" she begged.

"Just a minute," Martha responded grouchily. "I'm still missing six lines . . . five lines . . . "

"Oooh," Taranee cried as she blew out the two fireballs hovering over Will's bed.

"Hurry!" Will shrieked.

"Four . . . " Martha was saying. "Three . . . "

"I think the coast is almost clear," Taranee said. She grabbed Will by the elbow. Together, the girls darted out of the room and dashed towards the couch, where Irma and Cornelia were already sitting. Of course, they stubbed their toes on random boxes and pieces of furniture as they went.

"I hear a key in the lock!" Irma squeaked as Will and Taranee tumbled onto the couch.

"Two . . ." Martha said in the bedroom.

"Wait a minute," Cornelia pointed out. "This looks weird, doesn't it? All of us sitting here in the dark?"

Click!

Taranee jumped. That was Mrs. Vandom's key turning in the lock! Instinctively, she reached for a fragrant candle on the coffee table and touched its wick with her fingertip. With a sizzle, the wick burst into flame.

"One!" Martha announced triumphantly from the other room. At last, the humming and whining of the printer fell silent. And a brief instant later, the front door swung open into the dimly lit loft.

"Will?" Mrs. Vandom said. She poked her head through the door apprehensively.

"Um, hi, Mum!" Will chirped nervously from the couch.

"Hiya, Mrs. Vandom," Irma said, waving at Will's mother with a big, artificial smile.

Taranee gulped. She quickly looked around the loft. Had she missed a fireball? Did Will's mum somehow know that her daughter and her friends were . . . magical?

Uh, apparently not.

"Some storm, huh?" Mrs. Vandom said. She waved hello to the girls with a friendly smile. Then she walked away to stash her raincoat in the closet.

Taranee tried to see their group through Mrs. Vandom's eyes. Yup – they really *did* look like a bunch of ordinary teenagers, gabbing by candlelight. They'd totally gotten away with their supernatural shenanigans.

And if *that's* not magic, Taranee thought with a sigh, I don't know what is!

THREE

After Hay Lin left her friends at Will's apartment building, she began to hurry home. As she walked toward the Silver Dragon – the restaurant her parents had owned ever since Hay Lin was a baby – she found herself noticing each sidewalk crack she stepped over. She stared broodingly. Then, idly, she started tapping her right toe on each crack.

Before she knew it, her left toe was tapping the sidewalk cracks, too.

A minute later, Hay Lin had only moved half a block. And that's when she realised – she was dragging her feet.

Which would have been no big deal if Hay Lin had been, like, any other teenager. But she wasn't! She was . . . Air Girl.

She was famous for skipping, not tripping. Running, not walking. She was Miss Energy. Especially since she'd learned she was magical.

But today, Hay Lin's verve was completely vacant. Her heart just wasn't in it. The reason? Her grandmother was very sick.

If Hay Lin allowed herself to think about that, her vision began to blur and her lower lip started to tremble. So she *didn't* think about it.

She couldn't however, control the sadness that kept welling up in her chest. She couldn't even bring herself to step up her pace when the thunderclouds rumbling over her head finally opened up. While raindrops spattered her long, black hair, Hay Lin simply continued to plod along.

Finally, she reached the restaurant. It was closed for the break between lunch and dinner. The empty dining room felt eerily calm.

"Anybody home?" Hay Lin called out timidly.

There was no answer. So she headed for the stairwell next to the kitchen that led up to their cosy apartment.

"Mum? Dad?" Hay Lin called as she tromped up the stairs. "Are you there?"

When she reached the top of the stairwell, she heard her father's kind, quiet voice. But he wasn't talking to her. Her father was huddled in the middle of the hallway with a silver-mustached man.

It was Grandma's physician.

"What do you think, doctor?" her dad was asking.

Hay Lin shrank against the tea-green-coloured wall and held her breath. Her dad's back was to her. He didn't know she was there. But somehow, she couldn't bring herself to interrupt the conversation.

"Last month's flu weakened her quite a bit," the doctor admitted. "She's having a hard time recovering."

"I see," her dad said. He looked at his feet.

"The medication won't be of much help," he continued. "The truth is, your mother is simply very old. She seems tired, quite frankly."

The doctor gave her dad's shoulder a sympathetic squeeze as he added, "We'll continue with all of the treatments. Stay close to her! That's what she needs most right now – her family around her."

Hay Lin felt her mouth go dry as the doctor's

words registered with her. It sounded like he was saying there was nothing he could . . . nothing that could be done.

As her dad thanked the doctor, Hay Lin realised she was gasping for breath. The sound made the doctor peek over her dad's shoulder.

"Oh," he said. "Hello, young lady."

"Hay Lin!" her dad said. He spun around and regarded his daughter. His gaze traveled from her damp, puffy, blue coat to the puddle that was quickly forming around her shoes. "You're dripping wet! Go change, before you catch something."

Hay Lin tried to catch her dad's eye. She knew that the little bit of bluster was just a cover-up. Her dad was a big softie. And Hay Lin knew he was hurting inside.

I guess he's not ready to deal, Hay Lin thought, morosely. So she simply nodded.

"Okay, Dad," she said, kicking her purple ballerina slippers into the stack next to the stairs and unzipping her coat. Then she walked down the hall toward her room.

As she tiptoed past her grandmother's room, a wispy voice wafted out towards her. It sounded a lot like the gentle chirping of a cricket.

"A warm south wind would work better than a hair dryer, little one."

"Grandma!" Hay Lin said. She peeked nervously into the sickroom. Then she walked in, slipping her coat off her shoulders.

"Go on," her grandmother said, peeking slyly into the hallway to make sure the coast was clear. "Now that your father isn't around, let me see you use your powers."

For the first time that day, Hay Lin felt a little zing of happiness shoot through her.

Her grandmother plus magic, she thought with a little giggle. I guess that's the formula.

She tossed her coat and bag onto a chair and stood at the foot of her grandmother's bed. Then she closed her eyes and concentrated.

She imagined a cool breeze skittering across her cheeks. She pictured puffs of wind fluttering her grandmother's long, white hair. Hay Lin conjured up a friendly tornado, swirling around her.

And pretty soon, she felt the familiar *whoooosh* of a *real* tornado, swirling around her body.

It's happening, Hay Lin thought with a grin. Involuntarily, she swooped her arms over her head. She squealed as her damp pigtails spiraled around her torso and her plum-coloured miniskirt fluttered in the breeze.

Now here was the part that her grandmother couldn't see – which was too bad, because it was the best part.

The feeling.

Hay Lin felt sort of like she'd swallowed a million jet-puffed marshmallows. Or she'd suddenly become a bobbling balloon, barely tethered to earth by a string. Or she was living among the clouds.

She felt weightless – as light as air.

But then, as it always did, the magic began to dissipate. And when Hay Lin felt her pigtails – dry and silky now – plop back down over her shoulders, she knew the moment was completely over.

She opened her eyes and smiled at her grandmother.

"What do you think?" she asked.

"Ha-ha!" her grandmother cried. She clapped her feeble hands together. "Splendid!"

Hay Lin dropped to her knees next to the bed and smiled as her grandmother stroked her hair. Up close, she was startled by how sick her grandmother really looked. Her hair had gone wispy and thin. Her skin was pallid with illness. And her body looked tiny and weak inside her big, quilted, green robe.

Yet the cool, dry hand on top of Hay Lin's head felt powerful. As did her grandmother's words.

"I think you'll become very good, my little Hay Lin," she pronounced. Then she moved her hand to Hay Lin's cheek and gave it a pinch. "But first, you'll have to put on a few pounds, if you don't want the northwest wind to carry you off!"

"The wind is my friend, Grandma," Hay Lin giggled. Then she felt her face grow serious.

"How do you feel today?" she asked quietly.

"*Hmph!*" her grandmother said, looking even tinier as she scrunched back into the two fluffy pillows propping her up. "Let's just say that I've seen better days."

Then, as always, her grandmother turned the focus away from herself.

"And the other Guardians of the Veil?" she asked. "Are they well?"

"They're fine, Grandma," Hay Lin said. But

she wasn't really thinking about her friends. She suddenly felt something desperate and hard well up in her throat. And she couldn't hide the fear in her voice when she asked, "But you'll get better, won't you?"

"Of course!" her grandmother said, waving her skinny hand dismissively. "I foresee great improvement. Now, help me sit up, Hay Lin. There's something beneath my pillow."

Hay Lin jumped to her feet and held her grandmother's arm as the elderly woman leaned forward. Then, when her grandmother nodded at her, Hay Lin thrust her hand beneath the pillows. Her fingers touched something smooth and powdery.

"A scroll?" Hay Lin asked. She pulled out the rolled-up piece of paper. It was raggedy at the edges and yellowed with age. It was bound by a glinty brass ring.

"This is for you and your friends," her grandmother said quietly. "Give it to Will. She'll know what to do with it."

"Wh-what is it?"

"It's a map of the twelve portals, little one," her grandmother said. She settled back against her pillows heavily. "That is the number of openings in the Veil – the twelve passages that the creatures of Metamoor will attempt to cross through to reach our world."

Gulping, Hay Lin unfurled the delicate parchment. She blinked. She turned the big piece of paper over. Then she peeked over at her grandmother. Was Grandma losing her mind as well as her health?

"There's . . . nothing written on it," she said in confusion.

"Are you sure, Hay Lin?" her grandmother replied with a glint in her eyes that scrunched her crow's-feet into . . . a *lot* of wrinkles!

Hay Lin bit her lip and took another look at the "map." And suddenly, she felt the paper do a little shimmy in her hands. With a metallic, *zwing*ing noise, shadowy lines began to form on it.

"Oh!" Hay Lin squeaked. She gaped as the shadows grew darker. They seemed to pulse and expand, growing more complex with each passing second. The lines rounded and turned corners. Shadows scuffled into place around them. And suddenly, Hay Lin found herself looking at a familiar landscape – a city fanning out from an ocean beachfront surrounded by mountains on the other side. Rather than a dry street map, this looked more like an overhead photograph. Hay Lin could see the curve of every street, the rooftop of every unique building, even the little spit of beach that housed a black-and-white–striped lighthouse – a lighthouse Hay Lin recognised.

She'd visited that tall, fishy-smelling, cylindrical building on at least three school field trips. Each time, she'd yawned her way through some tour guide's nasal explanation: "This lighthouse is the oldest structure in Heatherfield. It has averted countless ship disasters, and today serves as a welcoming beacon to visitors from *blah, blah, blah, blah*."

"This is Heatherfield!" Hay Lin exclaimed. As she spoke, the final street and building shimmered into place on the parchment. Automatically, Hay Lin's eyes sought out her part of town. And she noticed that one building on the map began to pulse. Then it started to glow, turning a glimmery pink.

"That shiny point . . . ?" she said.

"Is your school gym, where your first battle took place," Grandmother confirmed. "That was the first passageway. The flames closed it up."

Then Grandmother reached over the map and put a bony finger beneath Hay Lin's chin. She turned her granddaughter's impish face towards her own aged one. Hay Lin found herself staring into her grandmother's rheumy eyes. She could see a dozen different emotions in those eyes – love, weariness, hope, nostalgia, and, most of all, resolve. Above all, even above her illness, Hay Lin knew that her grandmother was a very strong woman. And she seemed to be making every effort to pass that strength on to her granddaughter.

That was a lucky thing. Because her grandmother's next pronouncement chilled Hay Lin to the bone.

"But the next eleven portals," her grandmother informed her, "you and the other Guardians will have to close yourselves!"

FOUR

As Hay Lin spoke with her grandmother, someone was listening in. It was not an eavesdropping
parent or one of the many microscopic, otherworldly creatures that inhabited Yan Lin's bedroom, guarding her from evil.

No, it was the Oracle – the benevolent, all-
knowing being who had anointed the five
Guardians of the Veil. He was gazing down
upon the magical grandmother and granddaughter from the Temple of Candracar, the
mystical palace that floated in the heart of
infinity. The temple was suspended in a silvery
substance that was lighter than air and purer
than water.

Inside the temple, the Oracle strolled along
a pathway that hovered magically above a

lily-studded pond. The mazelike walkways were endless, as was the distance between the pond's clear, warm waters and the temple's ceiling. The walls that enclosed the pond merely seemed to soar up into infinity. They were also covered with the colours and figures of a thousand otherworldly artists. For it was only fitting that the minister of all things good and beautiful should be surrounded, at every step, with beauty.

The Oracle paused on the walkway and clasped his hands. Then he pulled his hands back into the flowing, bell-shaped sleeves of his long robe. Tibor – the ancient, stern man who always had and always would stand guard behind the Oracle's left shoulder – stopped as well. His silver hair and beard trailed down over his own long robes.

The Oracle's face broke into a peaceful smile. As the thoughts in his head became heavier, a flickering green window appeared in the air beside him.

Finally, the Oracle and Tibor began to watch over Hay Lin and her grandmother – his messenger from the Temple of Candracar.

The Oracle felt pleasure suffuse his being as

Yan Lin informed her sprightly little grand-daughter that the Guardians must close all the portals in the Veil themselves. Hay Lin, though daunted, did not lash out in fear or hostility.

The quavering Taranee or stubborn Cornelia might have responded differently, the Oracle thought. But that knowledge didn't crease his clear brow. For he also knew that Taranee, Cornelia, and all the Guardians would soon learn to accept their fates gracefully and to master their powers. He knew, even if they didn't, that magic was in their blood and in their bones. It was their destiny – their calling.

The Oracle returned his gaze to Hay Lin, who was curious about the map.

"The map doesn't show the portals," she was saying to Yan Lin. "How can anyone use it?"

As if she were speaking the Oracle's very thoughts, Yan Lin answered, "I've already told you and your friends – with time you will learn everything."

While Hay Lin continued to gaze at her grandmother quizzically, the frail, old woman bowed her silvery head.

"Yes," the Oracle said to the old woman,

with powerful waves of telepathy. "You may tell her. Tell her, Yan Lin, your story."

With a small nod, Yan Lin looked up at her granddaughter and spoke.

"Once," she said in her reedy, whispery voice, "I, too, was a Guardian of the Veil, long before you. And once I, too, was very impatient, just as you are now."

Hay Lin gasped and perched on the edge of her grandmother's bed, setting aside the precious map of Heatherfield's twelve portals.

"You were a witch, too?" Hay Lin asked.

"Witch?" her grandmother replied with a wheezy giggle. "That's not exactly a compliment! But it certainly is funny. We aren't witches. We aren't even fairies."

Taking Hay Lin's hand in her own, Yan Lin looked into her granddaughter's eyes and said, "We are something entirely different."

Hay Lin's sparkly, almond-shaped eyes widened.

"But in any case," Yan Lin continued, lightheartedly, "I don't know anything anymore. It's your turn now, Hay Lin."

It's a portent, the Oracle thought, of things to come.

The Oracle's musings – like the conversation between the elderly Guardian and the very young one – were interrupted by Hay Lin's father. He poked his head through the old woman's bedroom door. He was holding a bottle of dark liquid. "It's time for your medicine, Mother," he said. He stepped into the room and smiled. "And please, no fussing! I've tried it myself and it's very tasty!"

"If it's so good," Yan Lin shot back, "why don't you put it on today's menu?"

"Come on," her son chided. He took Hay Lin's place on the edge of the old woman's bed. "You don't want to make a scene in front of your granddaughter."

Yan Lin grimaced.

"Once I was the one who spoon-fed you, young man," she teased. "But it never crossed my mind to force something so nasty on you!"

"Very funny," the man said, pouring some of the amber liquid into a spoon and nudging it into his mother's mouth. She swallowed the elixir and made another face.

"See," Hay Lin's father announced. "That wasn't so bad, after all."

"Bleah!" Yan Lin said after she swallowed.

She stuck her tongue out like a child.

The gesture, at once so funny and so poignant, brought a surge of emotion to Hay Lin's heart. And the intuitive Oracle felt the emotion in his own. It was painful and bittersweet. He placed a cool hand on his chest and knew that its comfort was flowing earthward, into the heart of the young girl.

It worked. She smiled at her grandmother through her tears.

"Take care, Hay Lin," Yan Lin purred with a smile. "And don't forget, eat!"

"I promise," Hay Lin whispered. She leaned over and placed one simple kiss on the old woman's cool forehead. "Goodnight, Grandma."

Hay Lin walked out of the sickroom. She tucked the map – once again bound in its brass ring – safely into her coat pocket. The Oracle had seen enough. He waved his hand through the air. The pulsing, green window into his thoughts wavered until it was no more than a cloud of vapour with the faint scent of lemongrass and hyacinth.

Then he turned to his adviser, who bowed his gray, woolly head deferentially.

"And so," the Oracle announced, "the map

of the twelve portals has been delivered."

"Honorable Yan Lin has done truly excellent work, Oracle," Tibor responded.

"Yes," the Oracle said. "And this means her mission has been completed."

"I see."

"You know what to do, Tibor," the Oracle said. He strolled away from his adviser with a graceful gait that required no effort. "Inform the council of the congregation."

As the Oracle floated away, he pictured Yan Lin in the comfort of her soft bed, surrounded by the love of her family. After she passed away, she would rise through the heavens, effortlessly traveling through galaxies and dimensions. Eventually, she would arrive in the stadiumlike fortress of the council.

There, all the council members – from stalwart Tibor to even the volatile, wolflike Luba – would join hands and dance around Yan Lin. It would be a dance of celebration, of gratitude, of welcome.

"Yes," the Oracle murmured, as he glided through his beautiful temple. "She shall have the welcome she so greatly deserves."

FIVE

Cornelia tromped up the grassy hill, holding a
stick of smoldering incense out in front of her.
Its blue smoke smelled like sandalwood and
sea grass. She knew the scent was supposed to
be comforting, but it only made her nose itch.
She put a gloved hand over her mouth to stifle
a sneeze. Then she glanced behind her at her
friends.

Will's and Taranee's faces looked as stricken
as Cornelia felt. Will's knuckles were white as
she clutched her own stick of incense. And
Taranee, carrying a basket of snowy flowers,
was more trembly than usual.

Even Irma, Cornelia thought, a girl who can
always crack a joke, looks shaken. I guess
that's because this is one of the saddest

things we've ever experienced. A funeral – for Hay Lin's grandmother.

A cool autumn breeze whisked over the hill. Cornelia flicked a tear from the corner of her eye and clutched her white shawl tighter around her shoulders. Then, at last, the large crowd of mourners completed their long, slow climb up the hill to the pretty meadow where the funeral service would take place. In their all-white clothes, the people looked like a flock of somber birds.

"White is the colour of mourning in Chinese culture," Hay Lin had told Cornelia on the phone after she'd gotten the news about her grandmother. Her voice had been choked with tears. "The colour of snow."

And then Hay Lin had had to go help her parents. But before she'd hung up the phone, Hay Lin had told Cornelia something else. She'd informed her that her grandmother had also been a Guardian of the Veil in her own youth.

The news had shaken Cornelia.

So, not only, she thought, has magic suddenly invaded my life, but it's going to be a part of my life forever! I'm part of generations of Guardians. And someday, I'll have to pass the magic on to some unsuspecting teenager.

Unless you win the battle, a voice inside her said. If you conquer Metamoor's evil invaders, there will be no more need for Guardians. It's up to you, Cornelia. It's up to you . . . to you . . . to you. . . .

Cornelia tried to shake the pressure-cooker thoughts from her head and return her attention to the present. Several friends and family members were speaking to the group, saying affectionate, admiring words about Yan Lin. Out of the corner of her eye, Cornelia saw mourners' hands holding bunches of white blossoms. Others clutched ivory ribbons.

"The colour of snow," Cornelia whispered to herself.

She shivered as the funeral service neared its end.

Ribbons and flowers turning to snow, she thought. Yup, that makes about as much sense as anything else right now. I mean, how many more times will our lives change forever?

In school a couple of days earlier, everything had been normal. Well, as normal as it could be since the girls had become magical.

While the sun glinted off the tin roof of the Sheffield Institute, Cornelia had been hanging out with Will in the front courtyard. And she was enjoying the power that came with possession of a choice tidbit of gossip.

The instant Hay Lin, Irma, and Taranee had come into the courtyard, Cornelia blurted out, "Did you hear the news? It's got everyone at school talking!"

"What news?" Irma said. Cornelia couldn't help but relish – just a little bit – the envious frown on Irma's face. Irma was usually the one with all the news.

That's what comes from being a busybody, Cornelia had thought.

But what she'd said was, "The police are in the principal's office!"

Hay Lin gave a delighted shriek as the girls fell into step and headed for the front steps together.

"Poor Mrs. Knickerbocker," she'd said. "She's mean, but not *so* mean that she deserves to go to jail!"

Will snorted.

"Sorry to disappoint you, Hay Lin," Will said. "I guess that you didn't watch the news on

TV this morning, did you?"

"No, why?" Hay Lin gasped. "What did I miss?"

"It's even in the papers!" Taranee cried. "A boy from our school disappeared!"

Cornelia had sighed. Well, it looked like the gossip wasn't exactly hers to dispense, after all. But at least she could provide the missing boy's name.

"Andrew Hornby," she announced. "Do you remember him?"

"Who?" Hay Lin gasped, giving a little jump. "Do you mean that gorgeous blonde guy from the upper school?"

"Exactly," Will said. "He didn't go home for three days straight! As of last night, he's officially a missing person."

The group fell silent. Even Irma! Cornelia gave her chatterbox bud a sidelong glance. Irma didn't have one breathless remark to make? Not one clever quip?

Apparently not. In fact, Irma was looking a little freaked. Her usually rosy cheeks were sweaty and pale. She was gnawing on her full lower lip, completely wrecking her carefully applied cranberry-coloured lip gloss. Irma's silence wasn't lost on Hay Lin, either.

"Wake up, Irma!" Hay Lin said, giving her friend a nudge. She whipped a fat, felt-tip pen from the pocket of her slouchy, blue jacket and scribbled "Andrew" on her palm in purple ink. Then she held her hand before Irma's blinking blue eyes.

"Isn't that the one you're crazy about?"

"Well, yeah," Irma rasped. Then she'd skidded to a halt. The girls were in the school's foyer – still several feet away from their lockers.

"What gives?" Cornelia had sighed, glancing at her watch. "We're gonna be late for first period!"

"In any case," Irma said, her forehead furrowed with resolve, "I've been trying to tell you guys something."

As she spoke, an office door swung open behind her.

And that's not just any door, Cornelia had thought, catching her breath. That's Principal Knickerbocker's door! Taranee saw it, too.

"Look!" she'd gasped. "They're coming out!"

Dragging her friends with her, Cornelia had ducked behind a corner and peeked around it.

She saw the principal saying goodbye to two police officers. The men began to stalk away, looking heavy and official in their blue hats and bulky cop jackets.

"Thank you for everything, ma'am," one of the men said over his shoulder. "If we find out anything, we'll let you know."

"I'd appreciate that very much, Officer," Mrs. Knickerbocker said. "Good luck."

Cornelia looked down at Hay Lin with a grin.

"See?" she said. "They didn't take her away."

Hay Lin smirked.

"Maybe another time!" she said. Then she cackled mischievously.

"Hay Lin!" Mrs. Knickerbocker suddenly called out. She'd spotted Hay Lin and the others peeking around the corner! "I need to speak with you right away."

"Did she hear me?" Hay Lin asked her friends in a panicked whisper. They shrugged.

All Hay Lin could do was obey Mrs. Knickerbocker's order. Shooting her friends a terrified glance, she trudged into the principal's office. As Mrs. Knickerbocker waited inside her office door, she looked as imposing as ever. Her wispy, white beehive quivered on top of her head, and her tiny eyes looked even tinier behind her horn-rimmed glasses. As Hay Lin ducked past Mrs. Knickerbocker's bulky form, Cornelia heard her squeak, "I can explain everything, ma'am! It was only a little joke, and–"

"Sit down, Hay Lin. . . . " the principal began. Then she slammed the door shut.

What Cornelia knew now was that Hay Lin hadn't been in trouble at all. Mrs. Knickerbocker had just gotten a call from Hay Lin's father. And then, behind the closed office door, she'd had to break the terrible news to Hay Lin: her grandmother had passed away that morning.

Now, here we are, Cornelia thought sadly. While she'd been lost in her memories, Yan Lin's service had ended. The white-clad mourners began walking back down the hill. But Cornelia and her fellow Guardians lingered behind to wait for Hay Lin, who was giving her parents big, sad hugs. Hay Lin burst into tears and fell into her parents' arms.

If only we could use our magic to whisk away our pain! Cornelia thought. Then it might not be so bad having these strange powers.

Cornelia sighed and glanced at Will, Taranee, and Irma. They were standing next to her, looking miserable as they gazed at Hay Lin.

Does this magic thing freak them out as much as it does me? Cornelia had to wonder. I mean, I know Taranee is scared. And I have a feeling Will's a little weirded out that her powers are different from ours. And Irma . . . Irma is probably only as upset as she would be if they canceled *Boy Comet*.

But me, Cornelia thought, I've always had this need to have my life in control. I love that feeling of balance I get when I'm doing a perfect spiral in a skating routine. Or when my room is put together just the way I like it, even if the way I like it is in a total mess.

But now, she thought, I have control over nothing. Another round of tears welled up in her eyes. She looked down at her feet.

Everything was changing. Her best friend, Elyon, and Elyon's parents were missing. And now she was also mourning with Hay Lin for

Hay Lin's sweet, departed grandmother.

Nobody asked me if I wanted to be a Guardian of the Veil, Cornelia thought miserably. As self-pity washed over her, she saw Hay Lin approach their little group. Looking even smaller and wirier than usual, Hay Lin gave Will a tight hug.

"Thanks for coming, guys," she whispered in a raspy, small voice. "I love you all."

Cornelia opened her mouth to respond. But she couldn't think of what to say. And that distressed her, too.

I can't even be a good friend to Hay Lin, Cornelia thought, kicking angrily at a tuft of grass. Because, well . . . how can I be a good fellow Guardian when I don't even want to *be* a Guardian?

What's more, she thought with a sigh, ever since Elyon vanished without a trace, I have had nobody to talk to about all this.

Cornelia bit her lip as she thought of her best friend. Elyon had done more than vanish. Apparently, she'd also set a trap for Will, Hay Lin, and Irma. They'd been scared to death by some gruesome Metamoorian monsters!

For Cornelia, that was perhaps the most

bizarre part of all of it – that Elyon could betray her friends. Cornelia couldn't quite bring herself to believe that her best friend was capable of that.

No, she thought stubbornly. It can't be true.

As Cornelia told herself that, she became vaguely aware of Hay Lin extricating herself from her hug with Will. Hay Lin was peeking over Will's shoulder and blinking her teary eyes rapidly.

No, Cornelia thought again with a determined shake of her head. I just can't believe that Elyon's bad. Not–

"Elyon!" Hay Lin suddenly screamed.

"What?" Cornelia blurted out. She saw Hay Lin pointing to a spot down the hill. Cornelia spun around and followed her friend's gaze. She saw a knotty old tree, looming over a patch of dirt at the very edge of the cemetery. A few dried leaves rustled, and a couple of forgotten grave markers leaned against a wrought-iron fence nearby.

But Cornelia saw nobody, and certainly didn't see Elyon.

She gazed back at Hay Lin. She felt confusion and pain and dashed hopes roil in her gut.

But Hay Lin seemed still to be seeing something.

"It can't be!" Hay Lin cried. "Elyon!"

Cornelia turned to squint down the hill one final time. Again, she saw nothing. That nothingness made another round of tears flood her eyes.

It really can't be, Cornelia thought, morosely. Hay Lin must be crazy with grief – hallucinating. Nobody's there. Certainly not Elyon.

SIX

Elyon stood beneath a gnarled old tree. Under her feet, there was no grass. There was only dirt – lumpy with tree roots, bedraggled, neglected. A cold breeze rustled her straw-coloured bangs and blew her long braids this way and that.

And suddenly, Elyon realised something.

She'd never noticed the absence of cold! In Metamoor, that is, where she had been living for . . . a few days? A few weeks? Elyon blinked slowly. She didn't know anymore. And what did it matter? She was home now, in Metamoor, where she finally belonged, after years of exile here on earth.

She stopped to enjoy the rush of cool, damp wind on her face. It was good to feel the change of weather. In Metamoor, it was always beautiful. The sun shone steadily, the air smelled of sweet flowers. It was never too hot and never too cold. There was no inconvenient rain or ominous darkness. Of course, there were no thrilling thunderstorms, either. Nor was there any variety. . . .

Elyon shook her head lightly to halt her thoughts. She refused to feel nostalgia for the false life she had lived in Heatherfield. That would only give *them* what *they* wanted.

Elyon hummed a tuneless little song and closed her eyes for a moment. When she opened them, the thought was gone. She couldn't even remember what the thought had been. Only a hazy residue remained, as easy to wipe away as a day's worth of dust on a table.

She blinked her enormous blue eyes lazily and shifted in her knee-high boots. Their soles scratched loudly in the dirt. In fact, Elyon began to feel a heightened awareness of *all* the noises – beneath her feet and in the air. Caterpillars, undulating up the old tree trunk, made rustling, moaning noises that Elyon could hear distinctly. The last dewdrop of the morning – falling off a tree leaf onto Elyon's royal blue garment – landed with a heavy, audible plop.

This, Elyon knew, was her new magic. It had begun to burble up inside her.

A few moments later, all her senses – not just her hearing – began rising to extraordinary levels. The touch of a falling leaf glancing against her arm rippled through her entire body. The sun – glinting off faraway shafts of white marble – sparkled and danced in her eyes.

And that breeze! There were voices in it – the joyful call of songbirds flying hundreds of feet in the air and the soothing song of the dead beneath Elyon's feet.

Elyon was positively brimming with magic now.

And that meant it was time.

Elyon gazed up the hill. It was carpeted with a lush swath of verdant grass. She gave an-other lazy blink. Her mouth tightened into the smallest of smiles.

She didn't need to call attention to herself.

Her magic would call to *them*.

Them?

That would be her "friends" – the ones

Elyon had left behind, the ones now mourning beside an open grave. Elyon had watched impassively as Hay Lin hugged Will and said, "I love you all."

Though Hay Lin's voice was just a raspy whisper, Elyon heard it clearly. Hay Lin could have been just inches away, whispering in her ear, sharing a secret, the way she used to during science class at the Sheffield Institute.

Again, Elyon closed her eyes to the memory before it could even solidify in her head. Then she felt it leave her mind like a puff of vapour, swept away by the wind.

A good thing, too. Because Hay Lin had just spotted her. Elyon watched the skinny girl withdraw from Will's embrace and point at her.

Elyon smiled her tight, tiny smile.

"It can't be!" Hay Lin cried. "Elyon!"

A rustle of disbelief and confusion swept through the group. Elyon could feel their emotions thrumming through her own chest. She could feel Taranee clasp her hands in agitation. She could sense the buzz of confusion inside Irma's head. She felt hope lift in Cornelia's heart. And then she felt it die.

Because Elyon was no longer there.

Or, rather, she was invisible.

That was Elyon's magic at work. It had reached its height, vibrating and shimmering through her with incredible power. In fact, the magic was so strong it threatened to fly away from her, like a skittish bird.

Since she'd arrived in Metamoor, Elyon had been practising. Her mind had become increasingly supple. She'd learned to control her unwieldy magic – to catch it, mold it.

And now, her work had paid off. She had used her magic to will herself – her inconsequential body, anyway – into a state of invisibility.

Elyon was still there, of course. She felt the scratchy dirt beneath the soles of her boots, and she wiggled her nose as another breeze skipped playfully across it. But when she looked down at herself, all she saw was dirt and tree roots.

Her body was simply not there.

And that's what her *friends* were now telling Hay Lin. But Hay Lin was resisting.

"Elyon's here!" she insisted, pointing at the base of the tree.

"What do you mean?" Will asked. She

gazed down the hill, seeing right through Elyon. "Where?"

"She *was* down there," Hay Lin insisted. Her voice was still heavy with tears for her grandmother. "I saw her!"

Hay Lin ran a few steps forward and called out to her once more.

"ELYON!" she screamed.

Elyon did not answer.

Still, Hay Lin would not give up.

"She *was* there," she repeated to Will. "I swear it! She can't have hidden so quickly!" Will shrugged and glanced back at the rest of the group. "Let's go take a look," she proposed. She started down the hill after Hay Lin.

No, Elyon thought. She squinted at Will, focusing on her with all her energy.

No.

"Maybe," Will began to say, "it was only *uhhhnnn . . .* "

Suddenly, Will staggered. She squeezed her eyes shut. Her hand flew to her tousled red hair and clutched at her head.

Elyon watched Will falter. Will looked dizzy, and her face was screwed up with confusion and – perhaps – pain. Elyon felt a flicker of concern in her chest. But it was quickly extin-guished. Feelings like that belonged to the old Elyon. The one who had lived in Heatherfield.

As Will took a few unsteady steps back-wards, Elyon blinked with calm satisfaction. Will was moving away from Elyon's tree, away from her.

"Will, are you okay?" Taranee cried. All four friends turned to catch Will before her wave of dizziness knocked her over.

As Will's friends gathered around her, like a healing force field, Elyon watched – or did she feel? – the wooziness drain from Will's head.

Will's brown eyes slowly fluttered open. Her fingers unclenched, and she smoothed a hank of hair from her now damp forehead.

"Yeah," she muttered slowly. "I think I'm okay."

Elyon blinked again.

And Will gave Taranee a wan smile.

"Everything's fine," she sighed.

Cornelia glanced over her shoulder at the base of the craggy tree, the space still inhabited by Elyon's spirit. Cornelia sighed. And then she announced, "Let's go home, Hay Lin. You must have been mistaken. You're just upset."

The girls began to climb back up the hill, heading toward the lingering crowd of mourners. As she followed her friends, Hay Lin shot one final glance over her shoulder.

Hay Lin is a dangerous one, Elyon thought. She, more than the others, believes in that which isn't seen.

Smart girl, she thought.

Then she felt the magic burble up within her once again. This time, it gave form to that which had been formless. Her body, her pale blonde braids, her dress of rippling, silken fabric and billowing sleeves – all slowly became corporeal.

Elyon smiled. And this time, her smile was for real.

Because – in the same way that the magic had told her *their* thoughts and feelings – it now informed her that she was no longer alone.

Behind her was . . . he. Lord Cedric. Elyon didn't have to turn around to sense his presence or see his beauty. She envisioned his long, silky hair rippling in the breeze behind him. His crimson coat framed his square shoulders with perfect precision.

Cedric's sharp features were creased into a

smug smile. "Excellent, Elyon," he said, praising her.

A warmth suffused Elyon, like warm honey, like sweet satisfaction. She yearned to hear the words again.

And thus – she did.

"Truly," Cedric whispered, "excellent."

SEVEN

The day after Hay Lin's grandmother's funeral was a Sunday. And Will was relieved that she didn't have to dash off to school. There was no alarm and no panic. Sundays were for sleeping late.

But on Sunday morning, Will got up early. Why was it on the days that she could sleep late, she often woke up early?

Her mother was up as well and busy making waffles. Waffles were a good reason to get up early on a Sunday.

Not only were waffles served: so was "Mum-and-Will banter." Every time Will drowned her waffles in syrup, for instance, her mother made a crack about the high cost of maple products. Then she would suggest they move to the mountains to keep Will supplied with all the maple syrup her heart desired.

Next, Will would tease her mother about the fact that she – a grown-up! – never ate the crusts of her whole wheat toast.

And then the two would munch in silence while they read the Sunday paper. Will read the funnies and the sports section (she always checked it for any swimming news). Her mum grabbed the style section and read the front-page headlines out loud to Will.

As traditions went, Sunday breakfast was definitely not bad. In fact, Will had to admit, it was pretty nice. It was also one of the few times her mum relaxed completely, shaking off the stresses of that week's work at Simultech.

For a moment, on that particular morning, Will stopped to imagine how her mother would have reacted if she had known Will was a Guardian of the Veil.

Talk about stress! Will thought as she chewed a bite of waffle. One minute, I'm Susan Vandom's sorta slouchy daughter. I've got nothing to worry about but being the new kid at school. The next minute, I'm a magical being with the powers of the Heart of Candracar pulsing through my veins.

Will tried to imagine that as a normal thing. She saw herself putting on her jacket and heading for the door.

"See ya, Mum," she would call out. "I'm off to close another one of those pesky portals to the evil world of Metamoor."

"On a school night?!" her mum would protest.

"Well, y'know," Will would reply, "if I don't, the world as we know it will end. Total apocalypse. Kabam, kablooey, game over."

"Well . . . all right," her mum would allow with a shrug. "But as soon as you get home from saving the world, young lady, I want that biology homework done!"

As the daydream evaporated, Will realised the funny papers were crumpled in her fists. Her knuckles were white with tension.

"Whoa!" she whispered. She tossed the newspaper back onto the kitchen table.

"Has one of your comic strips taken a dramatic turn?" her mum asked with a wry smile.

Will gave a shaky laugh.

"Nah," she said, getting to her feet. "I think I might have had one too many waffles. I'm stuffed. Think I'll go for a bike ride."

"Good idea," her mum agreed. She got up from the table to clear their breakfast dishes. "Have a nice ride. I'm going to relax with a nice, postbrunch nap."

And I am going to keep my secret identity secret, Will thought as she went to her room to grab a jacket. I mean, first Mum and Dad get a divorce. Then Mum and I move to Heatherfield. Then I turn *magical*. It's way too much! The only thing that could make life more complicated right now would be Mum's knowing I'm a Guardian. She'd worry about me constantly. And probably ground me for life. Which would ruin everything.

As Will wheeled her bike out of the loft and into her building's elevator, her heart felt heavy.

The biggest bummer, she muttered to herself, is that none of this makes me care any less about being a newbie at Sheffield. Will sighed. When the elevator arrived at the lobby, she wheeled her bike out of the building. As she hopped on and started pedaling, her mind flashed to the first time she'd ever seen her magical self. She'd been riding her bike then, too. She'd seen her altered reflection in a shop window.

And her appearance had stunned her. As the keeper of the Heart of Candracar, Will had looked like an older teenager. Her usual uniform of slouchy jeans and sneakers had been replaced by striped tights, a midriff-baring purple dress, and rad, round-toed boots. But the most incredible thing had been Will's body. Not only had her back sprouted delicate, feathery wings, but all her flat planes had turned curvy. Her legs had lengthened and her waist had shrunk.

It had been the coolest.

Will steered her bike towards Heatherfield Park.

Naturally, she thought wistfully as she pedaled, there's no way anybody at Sheffield will get to see my cool alter ego. No, all they get is the real me.

Wait a minute, she thought. Before we all became magical, Taranee, Irma, Cornelia, and Hay Lin saw the *real* me. And they *liked* me.

The thought sent a happy shimmer through Will.

Then she pedaled through the arched gateway to Heatherfield Park. Almost instantly, the noise of the busy city streets disappeared, and Will was surrounded by the wonderful quiet of a Sunday. All she could hear was her bike tyres crunching through fallen leaves and joggers trotting around her.

She sighed contentedly.

Maybe, Will thought, this place isn't so bad, after all. The park is wonderful at this time of morning. The city seems so far away.

Will turned down a path and began to ride through a grove of trees. The trees were well on their way towards shedding all their leaves for the winter. The crisp, cool air smelled like mulch and wood smoke.

Suddenly, Will hit her bike brakes and skidded to a halt. In the branches of a nearby tree, she saw a group of boys.

"Uriah and his gang!" Will muttered. "What are they up to?"

Sheffield Institute's biggest bully definitely ruined the landscape Will had been enjoying. The redheaded, pimply-faced, pointy-nosed Uriah was perched on a thick branch. His thin lips were curled into a mischievous smile. He looked ready to pounce on something.

At the base of the tree were Uriah's friends – if you could call dudes who followed him around like puppies and obeyed his every order friends. Hulking, blonde Laurent was laughing his loud, donkeylike laugh and clapping his big, meaty hands together. Kurt – who was as short and tubby as Uriah was tall and skinny – rested his hands on his big belly and grinned up at the bully.

But Nigel – who had chin-length, silky brown hair and a kind face – was trying to be the voice of reason.

"I don't think this is a good idea, Uriah," he called up to the treetop.

"For the little gentleman," Uriah sneered, "nothing like this is ever a good idea. Chill out, Nigel! We're just having a little fun! If you don't try doing certain things at this age, when are you ever gonna do them?"

"Putting a dormouse in Martin's locker," Nigel retorted irritably, "is not what I'd call a 'little' fun."

Uriah's getting ready to catch a dormouse?! Oh, No! Will thought. She loved dormice almost as much as she loved frogs. The little, squirrel-like animals with the black masks over their eyes were really cute.

Will also knew that a dormouse in distress could cause some serious damage. And Martin Tubbs didn't deserve to have his locker ransacked by one, even if he was a total nerd who drove her friends crazy with his megacrush on Irma.

What was more, no dormouse deserved to be aggravated by the likes of Uriah!

Will gazed up into Uriah's tree. She could spot the little dormouse he was stalking, now. The poor thing was scampering around another tree branch, looking trapped and panicky.

Will felt her face go hot with anger. But she didn't make her presence known. Not yet. She had to act carefully. She knew Uriah was a big coward deep down. (After all, when he'd tried to vandalize Will's bike on her first day at Sheffield, one harsh stare from Cornelia had made him back down completely.) But still, there was no telling how he would react to a challenge from Will.

So she quietly walked her bike to a spot a few feet behind the gang and watched as Uriah tried to bag his prey.

"*Grrrr,*" Uriah growled as he made a grab for the little cutie. It darted easily out of his way and hopped to another branch.

"Mostly it's not fun," Uriah called down to Nigel, "because the stupid little critter won't let me catch him!"

But then, for once, Uriah came up with a clever solution. He suddenly grabbed the tree trunk and swung himself halfway around the tree. That caught the dormouse by surprise. The creature paused for an instant and flicked its bushy tail.

"Aha!" Uriah cried. "Gotcha!"

He grabbed the dormouse.

Will started to gasp. But then the dormouse slithered out of Uriah's grasp. In fact, the creature buried its sharp little teeth in Uriah's finger with a chomping sound.

"*Yaaaagggh!*" Uriah squealed. As he shook his hand wildly – with the dormouse still gnawing on his fingertip – he flailed himself right off the tree branch, and he landed loudly in a pile of leaves.

"Heh, heh, heh," Laurent giggled. "Now, this is what I call fun."

Uriah probably would have belted him if he

hadn't been so busy shrieking.

"*Aahhhh!*" he screamed again. Still lying on his back, he waved the determined little dormouse around his head. "Get it off me! Get it off me!"

Finally, Uriah gave his hand one last, mighty flail. It sent the dormouse crashing into the tree trunk! It slammed against the bark, then landed on the ground with a thud. As the little animal got to its feet, shaking its head blearily, Uriah gaped at his raw fingertip. Then he spotted a thick branch nearby.

He grabbed it.

He staggered to his feet and raised the branch over his head. All the while, he glared down at the disoriented dormouse.

"Why," he grunted, "you rotten little–"

"Don't you dare!"

The order had shot out of Will's mouth almost involuntarily! But when Uriah jumped back and dropped his weapon, Will knew she'd done the right thing.

At least, she *thought* she had. As Uriah's thugs all turned to glower at her, she started to have some second thoughts. Four to one – that was definitely a little unnerving!

Not that Will let on. She glared right back at the gang. Her fists were clenched, and her feet were planted firmly in the dirt.

"Ah, the new girl," Laurent said.

"So," Uriah sneered at Will, "what's your problem?"

"Leave the sweet thing alone," she shouted, pointing at the dormouse. The little animal was still staggering at the base of the tree.

"*Oooh,*" Uriah cried in a reedy falsetto. "I'm soooo scared. Look! I'm shakin' like a leaf!"

Then Uriah's expression returned to its usual threatening sneer. He thrust his greasy nose up at Will's.

"So, whaddya wanna do about it?" he growled. "This time, Cornelia's not here to get you out of trouble."

"For the likes of you," Will shot back, "I'm enough!"

"Oh, yeah?"

Uriah clenched his fists. Will clenched hers. And then, suddenly, she realised something.

She meant it! And she wasn't scared of this gang of guys anymore.

Why should I be? she asked herself as she took a threatening step toward them. I've got magical powers. I could kick all their butts with one wing tied behind my back!

Before Will could test the theory, Nigel stepped between her and Uriah.

"Hey . . . " he murmured. He put a firm hand on Uriah's shoulder and gave him a long look. It was half-placating, half-pleading.

And, at last, Uriah backed off. He pointed at Will and growled, "I'm not through with you!"

But even as he said it, he was scurrying toward the path. Naturally, his cronies fell into step behind him.

Idiots, Will thought. They get all tough with girls and defenseless animals. I swear I'll teach them a thing or two!

Rrrrrrrr.

The muffled whimper made Will jump. She'd almost forgotten about the true victim here – the dormouse! Will ran to the tree and crouched down next to the trembling critter. As she stroked its silky fur and tickled it comfortingly beneath the chin, she felt her anger melt away.

"So," she cooed to the sweet little dormouse, "how do you feel?"

The dormouse chittered again and blinked

its hazy, black eyes. Then it opened its mouth wide.

Aw, Will thought. It's yawning! Poor little thing must be exhaust–

Chomp!

"Ow!" Will squealed.

She wrenched her pinkie from the dormouse's needlelike teeth and clutched it painfully.

Or maybe it's just hungry, she thought with a groan. Then she gaped down at the dizzy dormouse.

"Hey!" she said. "Ungrateful little thing! I rescue you and this is the thanks I get?"

The dormouse, of course, ignored her and staggered a few steps away. But someone was listening. Someone in baggy red cords and big, boyish basketball shoes.

"Need a hand?" the boy's voice said playfully.

"You again!" Will said. She didn't bother to look up. She was too busy examining her sore pinkie and scowling.

I can't believe it! she thought as she grimaced through the pain in her finger. Uriah just doesn't know when to give up! Well, maybe *this* will help him see the light!

"I can manage, thanks!" she said. Then she slammed her fist down hard on the boy's big, sneaker-clad toe!

"Ow!" he cried. "What's your problem?!"

Will finally looked up at her tormentor.

Then she gulped.

The boy painfully clutching his foot was not Uriah.

In fact, he was a cute boy.

A *really* cute boy.

A really cute boy that Will recognised! He was Matt Olsen, the lead singer in an amazing band called Cobalt Blue. Will had seen him sing at the Halloween party only a few nights ago. He was a total hottie *and* a complete Infielder (as in, in with the most popular crowd at Sheffield Institute).

"Omigosh!" Will screamed. "Sorry! Sorry! Sorry! I . . . made a mistake! I . . . I thought you were someone else."

Matt painfully lowered his foot and glanced from the little dormouse to Will. Will smoothed her hair and staggered to her feet. She felt her cheeks flush bright red. Then she smoothed her hair back – again.

Real smooth, spaz, Will told herself. Now focus! He's talking to you!

"Dormice have a mean side to them," Matt said with a wry smile, "but you're pretty tough yourself!"

Okay, Will thought. This is *not* a good beginning. She decided to ignore Matt's teasing and . . . and what?! What should she say?!

Will imagined Cornelia rolling her eyes and dryly suggesting, "You could start by introducing yourself!"

"You're Matt, right?" Will said with a nervous smile. "I really liked you at the concert on Halloween."

Oh . . . my . . . God, Will thought desperately. Why don't you just come out and *tell* him you've been crushing on him ever since his concert. That would be *really* cool!

"That is," Will gulped, "I mean . . . I liked your singing!"

"Gee, thanks!" Matt said. He smiled again. But this time, it wasn't a wry smile. Or a sly smile. It was just . . . a sweet smile.

A really, really, cute smile, Will thought dreamily. She gazed up at Matt, who was tall and lanky and had a superstrong jaw dotted by just the right amount of scruffiness. He had perfectly tousled brown hair and a cool fisherman's cap and really nice hands. . . .

Oh yeah, Will remembered. I'm supposed to be introducing myself here.

"My name's Will," she said.

Matt gave Will a little nod – so cute! – and then pointed at the dormouse. He'd just stumbled into a tree root and fallen over with a tiny thud.

"And this is your pet, huh, Will?" Matt said. He crouched down to stroke the critter's fluffy tail. "Looks like it came out of hibernation a bit too early. Look how out of it the poor thing is!"

The dormouse chittered wanly and looked around in confusion.

"It's still stunned," Matt continued. "And cold and hungry, too." Will peered over Matt's shoulder at the animal.

Matt pulled out a woolly, orange sweater from his messenger bag.

"Here, it'll feel better with this," Matt said. In one deft motion, he scooped the dormouse into the sweater and rolled the wool up in a ball. In an instant, the critter was completely swaddled. Only its face poked out of the end of the bundled sweater. And that face looked very contented.

"It'll snuggle up inside," Matt said, getting to his feet with the dormouse in his sweater cradled in his arms. "And every once in a while, when it feels like it, it'll pop out to eat something."

Will gazed up at Matt's still smiling face.

His eyes are such a pretty brown, she was thinking. He smells like cedar. And . . . whoops, it's time for me to say something now!

"Um, looks like you know all about this stuff," Will said, nodding at the cosy little dormouse.

"My grandpa has a pet shop," Matt explained. "But don't ask me to take it over there! He's busy enough with all the animals he already has!"

With that, Matt held the dormouse out for Will to take.

That finally brought Will back to earth.

Wait a minute, she thought. Is Matt expecting me to take the dormouse home? Without authorisation from Mum? Does our new building even allow pets?!

"Hold on!" Will cried. "I can't keep it!"

"Are you kidding?" Matt said. "You two were obviously made for each other."

Will gazed into the little creature's eyes. The mischief in them had been replaced by a sleepy sweetness.

Rrrrrrr, the dormouse chittered.

Then Matt placed the animal in her arms. And Will felt something melt inside her. Despite herself, she began cooing to the dormouse.

Between this little guy and Matt, she thought dreamily, soon there's gonna be nothing left of me but a big puddle of mush. Ooh, right, Matt's talking to me again!

"See you at school," he was saying. When Will looked up, she felt a little zing travel through her. He was also writing something on a little card! Something that had to be . . .

"Here's my number," he said, handing the card to her. "If you need any advice on the dormouse . . . "

Will took the card. She looked at Matt. And then she blinked.

Here's the part, now, Will told herself, where you say, "Thanks!" Then you do something flirty or sassy. Something Irma-esque.

But Will's throat was too dry for her to talk. She merely smiled tremulously as he began to walk away. Before he got too far, he turned back around. He shot her another one of those really cute smiles. Finally, Will found her voice. Well, sort of.

"Bye!" she squeaked. Then she waved.

As Matt ambled off down the path, Will took a deep, long breath. Then she glanced down at the bundle of dormouse in her arms.

Rrrrooon, the critter cooed.

Finally, Will allowed herself to melt completely.

"Yes," Will whispered to the little dormouse. "I'm starting to like this city a lot!"

EIGHT

Irma sighed as she gazed into her bedroom closet. It was Monday morning – a crucial day in Sheffield Institute's social order. And what determined someone's standing in this complex system?

The outfit, of course.

But Monday's dress code wasn't as simple as wearing something supercool or stylish. No . . . that would be too easy. (And besides, supercool clothes were for Wednesdays, when everyone was making plans for the weekend.)

On Mondays, you had to dress with a weary air. Slouchy clothes meant you were tired. And *that* meant you'd been out all weekend, having fun. Maybe you'd had a date. Or you had gone to a bunch of parties. Or you had stayed out way past curfew at a concert.

If that was the case, you could lean against your locker Monday morning and say things like, "What a weekend. I'm exhausted!"

But you can't go overboard, Irma thought as she flipped listlessly through her clothes. If your outfit is *too* sloppy, you doom yourself to the dreaded "blending in." Nobody notices you. And by Tuesday, you're a nonperson. A totally unpopular Outfielder!

The thought made Irma shudder.

But only a little bit.

I can't believe, she thought, that only a week or so ago, *this* was my biggest worry. Now I have to, like, save the world from big blue monsters and stuff. Plus, I *really* have to tell my friends about–

"Irmaaaaa!"

Irma jumped. Could her dad's bellowing be any louder?

"You're late!"

"Coming! Coming!" she called. She turned back to her closet.

Finally, Irma shrugged and closed her eyes. She thrust both hands into the closet and grabbed two hangers. And when she opened her eyes, she was holding her favourite jeans and a pink sweater with a keyhole collar.

"Hey!" she whispered. "I should choose my outfits this way more often. This is the perfect cas-yet-cool Monday morning ensemble."

She hopped into the jeans and yanked the sweater over her head. Then she stepped into some funky, charcoal-gray clogs and grabbed a handful of hair bobs. As she hurried down the stairs, she whipped her hair into two pigtails and expertly pinned back a few tousled strands with some tiny blue barrettes.

Finally, she arrived in the kitchen. Her mum was just putting a carton of milk on the table next to a box of Irma's favourite cereal. And her dad was shrugging himself into his police sergeant's jacket and cap.

"Your breakfast, sweetheart," her mum said, retying the belt on her favourite orange bathrobe and smiling at her daughter.

Her dad, of course, was his usual Mr. Gruff self.

"Why aren't you ready?" he grumbled. "Why can't you ever manage to be on time?"

"But I *am* on time!" Irma declared, tilting her face up at her dad.

"Sure, it's the rest of the world that's early!" her dad said. He rolled his eyes and threw up his hands.

Irma rolled her eyes, too. But she couldn't help giggling at the same time. Driving her dad crazy was as much a part of her morning routine as brushing her teeth.

"Now drink your milk," her dad ordered, "and get out of here, on the double!"

Irma plopped down at the breakfast table and filled her bowl with Frosty Oats. Then she glanced at the milk carton. The sight of it made her cringe.

On the side of the carton was a picture of Andrew Hornby – glinting white smile, floppy shock of hair, cleft chin, and all. The words beneath the picture almost made Irma lose her appetite altogether: "Have you seen this boy? Blonde hair, green eyes . . . "

Irma shot a timid look at her dad as she poured some milk into her cereal.

"Any word about this boy? At the police station?" she asked in a small voice. Then she took a little bite of cereal.

"Not yet," her dad said. He buckled his holster around his thick waist. "But there's other news! Sergeant Sommer just told me a moment ago – the police in Aubry found the car of your friend Elyon's parents."

Her mum, who was standing at the sink, stopped drying the dish in her hand.

"Really?" she asked.

"Yep," her dad replied. "But there's still no trace of the girl or her family. Vanished into thin air!"

Her mum frowned while Irma gasped. Her cereal had suddenly turned to paste in her mouth. She could barely bring herself to swallow the mouthful.

"Aubry is pretty far from here," her mum said. "What were they doing all the way over there?"

"I'll let you know when I've read the report from the patrolman who found the car," her dad said. He pulled his cap more firmly over his brushy, blonde hair. Then he grinned at Irma and his wife and said, "See you later, ladies!"

"Be careful, Tom," her mum called.

Irma merely waved as her dad whisked out the door.

She took another bite of cereal and stared at Andrew's picture on the milk carton.

The plot thickens, she thought. Andrew's picture blurred as Irma began musing anxiously.

What *had* happened to Elyon? she wondered. Irma had no idea, but she knew it had to have something to do with the big, scaly meanies who had attacked her, Will, and Hay Lin in the gym.

If only her dad had known what she knew. He'd be searching for clues in science-fiction novels instead of police reports. But there was no way she could clue him in. He'd freak! Plus, he'd never believe her.

Irma and the other girls were on their own.

Which meant they needed to know this latest bit of information! Not to mention the *other* thing. The news Irma had been trying to reveal for days.

The thought of telling her friends her secret chilled Irma to the bone. But what choice did she have? She needed help – desperately. And her fellow Guardians were the only ones she could go to.

Twenty minutes later, Irma was walking with the four other Guardians into the school cafeteria. A couple of years ago, some seniors had converted a corner of the cafeteria into a coffeehouse. They even had a cappuccino machine! It was a great place to hang out, do homework, flirt with some hotties, and, of course, get your all-important caffeine fix.

But coffee was the last thing Irma needed today. She was jumpy enough. As the girls ducked through the cafeteria doors, Irma told them what she'd heard that morning.

"Aubry, huh?" Taranee said. "That's so wild! Do you think they were running away?"

"Could be," Hay Lin piped up. "But from what?"

"Who knows?" Cornelia said. "Even though we were in the same class together for three years, Elyon never told me much about her family."

Irma bit her lip as the group headed for a table near the window. Her friends were as clueless as she was! She slumped into a chair dejectedly. All this mystery was making her weary.

Will had the cure for that! The next thing she said made Irma jump.

"Maybe Elyon's disappearance and the disappearance of that boy are connected," Will proposed. "What do you all think?"

"That's a possibility!" Hay Lin said. She plopped down into the chair next to Irma.

"No, it's not a possibility!" Irma blurted.

She felt four pairs of eyes swing toward her.

"How can you be so sure?" Cornelia asked.

Irma felt a wave of nervousness flutter through her stomach. It was finally time to tell her friends what she knew. *Ugh* – why had she eaten two bowls of cereal? Her stomach was doing flips. This was going to be harder than she thought.

"I've been trying to tell you guys something for a few days now," Irma said. She heard her voice shaking a little. "But I really don't know how to explain it."

The girls blinked at her expectantly.

"I . . . I . . . know what happened to Andrew Hornby!" Irma cried.

"Whaaaat?!" Hay Lin squealed.

"So, why didn't you tell us before?" Cornelia demanded with a stern expression. Normally, this would have totally annoyed Irma. Cornelia was always criticising her.

But in this case, Irma thought guiltily, *I deserve Cornelia's scorn.*

"I didn't tell you," Irma admitted in a small,

squeaky voice, "because I was the one who made him disappear! But I didn't mean to. That is, I was going to undo everything!"

"Oh, no, Irma!" Cornelia said, rolling her eyes. "What kind of mess have you gotten yourself into this time?!"

"I really liked him – Andrew, you know – and he never even looked at me," Irma explained. She felt her skin crawl as her friends gazed at her in alarm. "And so . . . "

"And so?" Will prompted.

Irma heaved a big sigh.

"Well, it all happened around a week ago," she began. "Do you know the Zot, that disco near the square?"

Cornelia nodded. Of course, she'd been there. Cornelia had been *everywhere*. Irma tried to shake off her annoyance with Cornelia and continued.

"Well, they threw this big party," she said. "I knew Andrew was going. It was my chance to get him to notice me. And so . . . "

Will suddenly slapped her hands over her ears and beseeched Irma, "Don't say it. *Please* don't say it!"

"I transformed myself," Irma blurted. Then

she slumped over miserably, dropping her fore-head on the cafeteria table.

"She said it!" Will cried.

Irma felt awful.

Why, why, why, she wondered, is the right decision so clear in hindsight? At the time, it seemed like no biggie at all.

In fact . . . it had been fun.

"My parents had been asleep for awhile," she told her gaping friends. "All I had to do was think about it, and I changed my appearance."

Irma couldn't help feeling an electric thrill tingle down her spine as she remembered her second transformation into her magical self.

She'd simply stood at the foot of her bed and looked down at her slightly plump, short legs, her slouchy sweater, and the choppy ends of her wayward hairdo. Then she'd wished them all away. Instantly, she'd been surrounded by a whirl of magical energy. It had been so power-ful it had whisked her clothes away. Irma had thrown her arms into the air as her body grew lean and willowy. She'd felt her flower-petal wings emerge from her back. The entire trans-formation gave her an enormous sense of power. And freedom.

Because there was no denying it. The magical Irma was gorgeous. Her blue eyes had gotten bigger and they winked coyly. Her hair was silky and arranged in a perfectly sleek do. And her figure was lithe and completely curvy.

"I hid my wings under a shawl," Irma said, "and I sneaked into the party."

She felt less guilty with each word. She just couldn't forget how thrilling it had been. And how fun!

"You should have seen it," she said breathlessly. "I was the center of attention!"

"Including Andrew's?" Cornelia asked.

"Especially his!" Irma said. "We talked and danced all night. It was fantastic!"

Hay Lin – never known for her boy-craziness – huffed in exasperation. "I can't believe it!" she sputtered. "You used your powers for a party?!"

"I didn't think I was doing anything wrong," Irma protested.

"And then?" Will sighed. "Get to the point, Irma!"

"Right," Irma said. She felt her face redden and her breath quicken. Here came the really awful part!

"So, in the end, Andrew offered me a ride home in his car and I accepted," she explained. "But he wanted to pull a fast one! He parked the car in a dark place and he tried to kiss me!"

"And you?" all four friends cried at once.

"You really want to know?" Irma squeaked. "I . . . uh . . . turned him into a toad!"

Irma still felt panicky as she remembered Andrew's sudden transformation. Make that transformations. First he'd gone from sweet, cute, boyfriend material into a leering, lecherous guy. And then he'd gotten a funny, bug-eyed look on his face. He'd uttered one final word: *"Ribbit!"* Then he'd morphed into a green, warty, springy-legged toad.

"He got scared, jumped out the window, and disappeared," Irma confessed. "I followed him! I looked for him. But it was useless!"

There! Irma's shameless story was out on the table. Her friends could commence hating and ostracising her now.

Irma sighed and hung her head, awaiting her fate.

Pffffftt.

Huh? Irma looked up at Hay Lin. She was covering her mouth with her hand. Her eyes were a little watery and *very* smiley.

Snorrt!

This time it was Will who was covering her mouth. She was definitely trying to suppress a giggle.

But it was Cornelia who finally threw her head back and started laughing. That, of course, set off a chain reaction.

"*Waaaah-ha-ha-ha!*" Hay Lin finally gasped.

Taranee and Will collapsed onto the table in uncontrollable, heaving giggles.

Well, this is unexpected, Irma thought. And . . . totally wrong!

"What are you laughing about!" she gasped. "This is serious! I feel terrible! It's a tragedy! A catastrophe!"

That, of course, only made her friends cackle even harder. Cornelia was wiping tears from her scrunched-up blue eyes, and Taranee looked as if she were having trouble breathing.

Okay, somehow this is *not* making me feel any better, Irma thought, crossing her arms irritably over her chest. In fact, the only thing that could make this whole scene any *more* annoying would be – Martin Tubbs.

And, of course, there he was – Martin

Tubbs. Geek extraordinaire. And madly in love with Irma. Martin always seemed to show up at the precise moment that Irma did *not* want to see him. Which was, well, pretty much always.

But *especially* now, when her friends were making fun of her in the biggest way.

She glanced at Martin. He was looking even more dorky than usual in a backwards baseball cap, V-necked sweater, and his usual Coke-bottle glasses.

"Martin," she growled, "disappe–"

"NO!" screamed her friends suddenly. Will and Taranee leaped across the table to restrain her, while Hay Lin slapped her hand over Irma's mouth.

Oh yeah, Irma thought, remembering the toad issue at hand.

As lovely as it might be to make Martin Tubbs *really* disappear, that would only add to her magical problems.

So Irma composed herself. She shook off her friends and turned to Martin with a big, sugary, and totally fake smile.

"Um, would you be so kind," she said, "as to shove off?"

Martin grinned.

"Your wish is my command, sweet thing," he said. Then he trotted off to class.

Close call, Irma thought. She felt weariness suffuse her being once again. And I thought being magical was going to make life easier!

NINE

Taranee walked with her friends towards the cafeteria exit. She couldn't stop staring at Irma. She didn't know what she found more amazing – the fact that Irma had used her magic to turn a boy into a toad, *or* that she'd had the courage to whip herself into her magical form and go to a disco, all by herself!

The idea of it catapulted Taranee into shivers of shyness.

But then, as she watched Irma plow through the cafeteria's double doors, another thought suddenly occurred to her.

Hey, she thought. Why *couldn't* I do that? After all, I'm just as magical as Irma. I can whip fire out of thin air! If I can do that, I can certainly take my magical self to a party.

Taranee tried to imagine herself in her magical uniform – tight, striped leggings and slim halter top, her beaded braids transformed into an awesome updo. She pictured herself making friends with a crowd of cool kids she'd never met, dancing confidently to the music, telling jokes that sent everyone in the room into gales of laughter.

Then she pictured her glasses flying off as she spun around the dance floor. After that, she would trip blindly over a chair and spill soda all over her Guardian clothes!

Taranee cringed. Then she couldn't help giggling at the image.

"Hee, hee," she whispered to herself. "Okay, I guess I still have a ways to go. And banding together with my friends on this Elyon/Andrew mystery is as good a place to start as any."

Taranee returned to the conversation.

"And so?" Irma was asking as the group tromped into the courtyard. They had to cut across the square to get to Sheffield's main building for class. "What do we do?"

"Simple," Will said. "We have to find Andrew right away and . . . *uhnnn!*"

Taranee gasped. Will was clenching her forehead and staggering blindly. Taranee caught Will's trembling arm before she could tumble into the grass.

"Will!" she cried. "Are you having that funny feeling again? Should we start worrying?"

Will looked as pale and trembly as she had after Hay Lin's grandmother's funeral. She blinked with heavy eyelids and breathed, "It's like a shiver. Dizziness. Like I'm falling into nothingness!"

"No!" Hay Lin suddenly said.

Taranee spun around in surprise. That was kind of harsh! Then she realised Hay Lin wasn't talking to Will. She was pointing to a pink stucco wall at the far end of the courtyard.

"Hay Lin?" Cornelia said.

"Look!" Hay Lin screamed. She pointed wildly at the wall. "This time it's not my imagination!"

Taranee and the others looked at the wall. Collectively they gasped.

"Elyon!" Cornelia cried.

Hay Lin was right. This time it *wasn't* her imagination. Taranee could see Elyon clearly. She was dressed in a royal-blue suit with a fluffy, grey, cowl neck. She had one hand propped casually on the wall. But her face was anything but casual. She was staring at the girls coldly.

And then she did something – magical.

"Omigosh!" Hay Lin cried. "She's going right through that wall. She's a ghost!"

Taranee squeaked as her gaze shifted from Elyon's cold glare to her arm. Elyon did indeed seem to be half-disappearing into the hard, stucco wall!

And Elyon didn't stop there. Now she was shifting sideways. The entire right side of her body melted into the wall. Taranee held her breath. What was going to happen next?!

Then Elyon's face began to look desperate. She lifted her hand toward the girls. And then, she disappeared through the wall entirely.

Taranee started breathing again – make that hyperventilating – while her friend sprang into action.

"It's like she's calling to us," Will said. "Maybe she wants to tell us something!"

"Let's follow her," Cornelia yelled.

Will, Hay Lin, and Irma didn't hesitate. They began to rush across the courtyard to the wall where Elyon had disappeared.

"W-w-we can't just leave!" Taranee found herself whining. "We still have classes!"

"Oh, puh-leeze!" Irma said. She was grinning as she dashed across the grass.

"Seriously," Taranee said as she chased after her friends. "If Mrs. Knickerbocker catches us, there's going to be trouble!"

Taranee could just picture her no-nonsense mum learning that Taranee had skipped out on school. Somehow, Taranee didn't think she'd believe her excuse: "Oh, Mum, I just *had* to ditch class. The ghost of my friend Elyon stopped by the school yard!"

Taranee rolled her eyes and looked longingly over her shoulder at the crowd of kids streaming into Sheffield for the day.

Then Cornelia's voice made her jump.

"The principal will never find out," she assured her. Then she spoke to the group. "Step aside, ladies. I'll open an emergency door."

Cornelia gritted her teeth and thrust her palm toward the wall. Suddenly, her hand began shaking.

And glowing!

Green, vibrating rings of energy began pulsing out of her palms. Taranee didn't know how Cornelia was wielding this power any more than she understood her own sudden ability to conjure up fire.

All she did know was – it worked!

A huge, circular hole suddenly appeared in the thick, stone-and-stucco wall.

"Whoa!" Taranee gasped as the girls began to scramble through the opening. After she herself had clambered through the hole, she asked Cornelia, "And do you know how to close the emergency door?"

"Sure," Cornelia said with a shrug. "It's all a question of concentration. All you have to do is think about it really hard and–"

Cornelia closed her eyes and tried to zap the wall shut again with her magic vibes.

But when she opened her eyes, the hole was still there! In fact, now it was more than just a hole! It was a jaggedy gash that extended all the way to the top of the wall! An absolute chasm!

Cornelia cringed. Then she shrugged and grinned at her friends.

"Okay," she tittered. "So I still need a little more practise."

"We're in for it," Taranee said, rolling her eyes.

"And on top of that," Hay Lin observed as she looked up and down the street, "we've lost Elyon, too."

Will shook her head.

"Let's go," she said. "There's only one place where we can hope to find her. And that place is her house!"

Cornelia nodded in agreement, and they began to hurry down the street toward Elyon's house. But Taranee hesitated for a moment. She peered back through the hole in the wall, scanning the school yard for a sign of Principal Knickerbocker's bouncing white beehive. The courtyard was empty and it looked as though they really had escaped without notice.

We *are* the Guardians of the Veil, Taranee thought desperately. We *have* to go look for Elyon. She's part of this whole battle between good and evil.

"And, hey," she whispered to herself as another thought suddenly occurred to her. "Maybe someone in Candracar could write me an excuse note!"

The idea made Taranee giggle again. Then

she began dashing down the sidewalk after her friends.

"Wait for me," she called.

Ten minutes later, the girls were tiptoeing across Elyon's lawn. Her big, grey house looked utterly abandoned. Every window was dark, and the grass was already becoming long and unruly. Irma led the girls around to the back-yard.

"This way," she said in a hushed voice. "It looks like the backdoor is open!"

Without even hesitating, Irma, Cornelia, Hay Lin, and Will ducked through the door. Yet Taranee couldn't bring herself to step over the threshold. As the girls made their way into the kitchen, Taranee clung to the doorjamb.

"Are we really sure of what we're doing?" Taranee asked. "This is called unlawful entry. My mother is a judge, and my father is a lawyer, and I know for sure that the people who do these things get locked up!"

"If you don't feel up to it," Cornelia said slyly, "no one's forcing you. Wait for us out here."

Taranee blinked at Cornelia. Then she

glanced over her shoulder at the windswept, and very empty, backyard.

"You want me to stay out there all alone?" she squeaked. "Forget it!"

Cornelia giggled.

Great, Taranee thought as she shoved the backdoor closed with her foot. Cornelia's totally manipulating me into breaking and entering. Let's just hope she can manipulate me out of trouble if we get caught.

She followed her friends through the kitchen and into the living room.

"Wow!" Hay Lin breathed. Taranee gasped, too. The place was sort of creepy. The ceiling seemed to loom several stories over their heads. It was dotted with ornate chandeliers with red crystals. Underfoot was a sumptuous Oriental rug. And covering the windows were heavily swagging red velvet curtains.

"It looks so much smaller from the outside," Hay Lin said.

"Which way do we go?" Will wondered aloud.

Frup, frup, frup, frup.

What's that sound? Taranee asked herself. Then she saw Will pointing at the ground.

"Look!" she screamed. "Footprints!"

That's exactly what that sound is, Taranee thought. Then she gasped as she actually saw the footprints scurrying across the hardwood floor. She could see the imprint of invisible shoes scuffing the floor. She could even see little billows of dust rise with each step.

The only thing Taranee couldn't see were the feet that were making the footprints. Those were invisible!

The footprints weren't just appearing randomly. They were walking with a purpose.

Right toward a door beneath the staircase.

"Looks like a clear invitation to me," Will announced, following right on the footprints' heels. Will opened the door. It swung open with an eerie *creeeeaak*.

"It's the basement," Will told the others.

Naturally, Taranee thought dryly, the footprints would take us to the creepiest part of the house.

Will peered into the gloom of the basement. Taranee peeked over her shoulder. But she couldn't see a thing.

"Give us some light, Taranee," Will said.

"With pleasure," Taranee replied.

She closed her eyes and cupped her hands out in front of her. Then she felt something warm form in her hands. In fact, the warmth extended all the way up her arms, settling finally in her chest.

The feeling was so lovely Taranee had to smile. Then she opened her eyes. When she did, she saw a huge swirl of fire curling out of her hands. The fireball floated upwards until it stopped just beneath the basement ceiling.

The room – a big, empty, circular cavern of a space – was completely illuminated.

And for the first time since she'd arrived at school that morning, Taranee forgot to feel scared. For the first time, she realised something: her magical powers were just that – powers!

The thought filled Taranee with determination. And this realisation made it just a little easier for her to square her shoulders and follow her friends down the stairs into Elyon's mysterious basement.

TEN

As the fireball floated out of Taranee's palm, Cornelia stared into the basement.

There was no sign of the footprints anywhere. No, it was just Elyon's same old, looming basement. Whenever Cornelia had spent the night at Elyon's house in the past, she'd avoided the basement. It was creepy. It looked like the inside of a giant tin can. The walls were gunmetal grey and perfectly curved. The floor was stubbly cement. And except for a few boxes scattered next to the curving staircase, the high-ceilinged room was perfectly empty.

Now Cornelia drifted down the stairs in a haze. As she walked, she sifted through her memories, trying to remember each time she'd come over to Elyon's house.

Had she ever noticed a glimmer of magic there before?

Cornelia pictured wan, wispy-haired Elyon and her sweet, ordinary parents. Nothing about them seemed magical or sinister. Elyon's parents didn't even seem that interesting. (But that was kinda normal, too. They *were* parents, after all.)

No, Cornelia decided. If Elyon was magical, like Cornelia and the other Guardians, she must have been as oblivious to it as they'd once been.

Cornelia shrugged sadly.

Then again, she thought, what difference does it make? Elyon's gone now, anyway.

The thought filled Cornelia with emptiness as she reached the basement floor with the rest of the girls. They all began gazing around the basement in confusion.

"There's no sign of the footprints," Irma said.

"And this basement has no doors," Will added. "Where were they trying to lead us?"

An echoey, ghostly voice came from behind them.

"To me, girls."

Cornelia gasped and spun around. It was

Elyon! She was pressed against the far wall of the basement. Her eyes were wide and soulless, and her arms were outstretched.

"Come to me," she intoned.

Will took one halting step forward while Irma and Taranee cringed behind her. She peered at Elyon, who stared back at her blankly.

"Elyon!" Will said hesitantly. "Can . . . can you hear us?"

Elyon's only reply was the same monotone phrase.

"Come to me," she said. "Come to me."

As she spoke, Elyon's body began to melt into the wall behind her! She drifted through the wall, the way smoke disappears into the air. Cornelia barely realised Elyon was melting away until Elyon was almost gone! In a few seconds, only her face and her outstretched arm were visible.

"Come to me," she whispered one more time.

And then she disappeared.

Cornelia ran to the wall and banged her fist against it angrily. The thump made a hollow, metallic *dong*ing sound.

"Another wall!" she said. "This is becoming a habit." She could hear a desperate catch in her own voice. She hated the sound of it! And – for a moment, anyway – she hated Elyon for making her feel so confused. And helpless. And . . . sad.

Where had Elyon *gone*?

Cornelia tapped on the wall some more. It was clearly some kind of metal. The wall was made of huge panels of metal, wedged together with rough seams.

"Let me take a look," Irma offered. She stole up next to Cornelia. She began scratching at the seam next to the spot where Elyon had melted away.

"Hey," she said. "It's not solid, after all. I can see . . . there's a door behind all this."

Cornelia peered over Irma's shoulder. Irma was right. Cornelia could see the edges of an entryway between the metal plates.

A doorknob, or a way to get beyond the plates, was nowhere to be seen.

"Looks like it's sealed," Irma said. "There's no way to open it!"

Cornelia jumped. She could open it. She had the powers of the earth within her! She could manipulate matter with nothing more than an impulse and her new magic.

Cornelia couldn't help remembering her gaffe in the school yard only a few minutes before. While blasting a huge hole in the wall had been a cinch, closing it up had been a disaster. She'd ended up destroying half the wall.

She had laughed it off at the time, but deep down, the mistake had filled her with panic.

Cornelia was used to getting good grades at school. Her ice-skating routines were precise and perfect. She almost never fell. And as for her look – she made sure she never had a blonde hair out of place. She liked being in control.

And now, she was far from in control. Her magic felt like a skittish horse that she hadn't tamed yet. If it failed Cornelia again, Elyon might drift farther away still.

And the mysteries facing the Guardians would only deepen.

I want some answers! she thought. And I think Elyon knows something.

Feeling confidence rise within her again like bolts of energy, Cornelia said to Irma, "No need for opening the door. All we have to do is – step aside, Irma!"

She didn't have to ask Irma twice. As Cornelia reared back, feeling green bursts of magic build up in her fingertips, Irma scurried out of the way.

Cornelia gritted her teeth.

She focused every ounce of her mental strength upon the metal plate.

And then, she gave it a magical *zap*!

Just as she'd hoped, the huge, heavy plate toppled toward her with a creaky roar. As Cornelia jumped nimbly out of the way, the plate crashed to the cement floor with a thunderous *briiingggg*!

There was now a gaping hole in the wall.

"Whoa!" Hay Lin cried. She scampered over the plate and jumped through the hole. The rest of the girls followed. As Cornelia walked over the fallen slab of metal, stamping her feet for emphasis, she saw that there was a green hieroglyphic on the door.

"Huh?" she said, gazing at it curiously. It was a green circle with a slice cut out of the center in the shape of a backward *C*. On top of the circle was a long, thin triangle. Beneath it was another triangle. But this one was short and squat.

Cornelia shrugged and hopped through the opening she'd made in the wall.

"Whoa!" she heard Hay Lin say again. But this time, she spoke in an awed whisper.

They had entered an enormous, endless cavern!

Actually, it wasn't really a cavern, since it was clearly manmade. (Or creature-made, Cornelia thought, with a shudder.) The long, shadowy tunnel was paved with slabs of marble and lined with pale bricks. Hanging from the walls were yellow lightbulbs, all of which were faintly, eerily glowing. Over the girls' heads were successive arches made of dark, red brick. And beneath their feet was the same green symbol Cornelia had noticed on the door. Except this time, it was about twenty feet long!

This sort of feels like a big, long throat, Cornelia thought, right down to that funky, moist smell in the air. It's like a combination of mold and stagnant pond water. *Ew!* Now I know what it's like to be swallowed by a whale!

"What is this place?" Will wondered aloud.

"If it's a broom closet," Hay Lin whispered, "it's the weirdest one I've ever seen."

As Hay Lin gazed over her head in wonder,

she didn't seem to notice – as Cornelia did – that something *very* odd was happening in Hay Lin's jacket pocket. It looked . . . it looked as if flames were shooting out of the pocket! But there was no scent of smoke in the air, and Hay Lin's blue jacket didn't seem to be burning.

Before Cornelia could cry out, Taranee grabbed Hay Lin. Fire, after all, was her turf.

"Your jacket!" she shrieked.

"*Aagh!*" Hay Lin cried. But then she closed her mouth and nodded her head.

"Oh, yeah," she muttered. Fearlessly, she plunged her hand into her pocket. When her hand emerged, the flames had disappeared. Instead, Hay Lin was holding a folded piece of paper. It looked aged and yellowed. Its edges were roughened, and the paper was so worn it was practically transparent.

"Whew!" Hay Lin breathed as she unfolded the paper into a huge square. "What a relief. It's my grandmother's map. The chart of the twelve portals!"

"Where did that come from?" Will exclaimed, looking at the map. "And why didn't you tell us about it?"

"I was going to, but with everything that's

happened, it completely slipped my mind," Hay Lin said.

The girls crowded around her to peer at the paper. Cornelia could see the familiar shape of Heatherfield's beach. Drawings of two big buildings not far from the beach were pink and glowing.

"It's a map of the city," Taranee said, realising what the map was showing. "And these shiny points . . . ?"

"They're the passageways leading to Metamoor," Hay Lin explained. "The portals that we have to close. The first was the one in the gym."

"And this other one?" Will piped up, pointing at the other glowing building. It was a few blocks away from Sheffield on the map.

As soon as Will asked the question, Cornelia knew the answer. She recognised the glowing house on the map. And as she did, her heart sank and an oppressive buzz began to fill her head.

She felt as if she were suddenly moving in slow motion as she watched the realisation dawn on the faces of her friends.

Only Will had the strength to say the truth

out loud. "It's Elyon's house!" she cried, pointing at the shiny point of the map. She looked at her friends desperately. "We're inside the portal!"

The moment the words left Will's mouth, the dank, scary passageway filled with a low rumbling – a rumbling that quickly morphed into a roar.

The floor began to shake beneath the girls' feet. Puffs of dust sifted down from the vibrating brick ceiling.

And then – with a horrible, wrenching boom – something erupted out of the floor! It was a new wall! It unfurled from the marble tiles like a hard-edged snake. Then it shot up towards the ceiling until it hit the top of the tunnel with a slam. Next, the wall widened, expanding until it struck one side of the tunnel, and then the other.

In an instant, the wall had sealed the tunnel shut.

"It's a trap!" Will screamed.

That's exactly what it is, Cornelia thought. She looked around wildly, searching for a solution, for a way out, for . . .

For Hay Lin.

Cornelia saw Will pounding on the fresh, new brick wall. She saw Taranee wringing her hands in terror. And she saw Irma spinning around in confusion.

But Hay Lin was nowhere to be seen.

That's because, Cornelia realised in alarm, she's caught behind the wall!

Will, Irma, and Taranee all seemed to realise it at the same time Cornelia did. And all three of them turned to her for a solution.

"Cornelia!" Irma shrieked at her. "Do something!"

Cornelia gazed at the wall. It was imposing, impenetrable, and made of solid brick! It would be much harder to crack than Sheffield's stucco walls or even the metal plates in Elyon's basement. She felt her breath coming in short, shallow gasps.

She didn't understand any of this.

Was Elyon trapped behind the wall, too? Or was Elyon the one who'd created the wall?

Had she been taken away from them?

Or had she betrayed them?

The only thing that Cornelia *did* know was – Elyon was not the friend Cornelia had thought she'd been.

Hay Lin, on the other hand, was a part of W.i.t.c.h. And a true friend.

There's no way I'm going to lose *her*, Cornelia thought. I've *got* to save Hay Lin. And I'm going to do it with my magic.

And for the first time since she'd gotten them, Cornelia felt grateful for her magical powers. She felt energized by them. And, yes, in control of them.

Without hesitating for another instant, she stalked over to the wall and thrust her arms out before her.

"Move back!" she barked to her friends. "I'm going to knock this wall down!"

ELEVEN

Hay Lin screamed as the brick wall suddenly burst up through the floor.

She felt her grandmother's map slip from her trembling fingers. And she watched the stunned faces of her friends – all four of them – disappear.

Trembling, Hay Lin gazed up. She watched the wall connect to the brick ceiling with a dusty groan. She screamed again and began running to her right. But it was no use – the wall had hurtled outward as well as up. It sealed the tunnel shut. On both sides.

There was no way around it.
Hay Lin was trapped.
Alone.

Drawing in a deep, shuddery breath, Hay Lin screamed one last time.

"*Aaaaaah!*" she cried, throwing herself against the wall. The bricks were cold and smooth, like a reptile's scales. But they were also hard, unyielding, impenetrable. Hay Lin couldn't hear a single sound from the other side of the wall. It was as if her friends had suddenly just been swallowed up.

Then Hay Lin realised something – it was actually the other way around. *She* was the one who had been snatched away, who had disappeared.

The face of her grandmother suddenly flashed through Hay Lin's mind.

But her grandmother's face was quickly replaced by the sight of red spots. She was so afraid, she was becoming half-blind!

Hay Lin squeezed her eyes shut and pounded on the wall, sobbing.

"Get me out of here!" she shrieked.

"What are you afraid of, Hay Lin?"

The voice – Elyon's voice – was right behind her. Hay Lin felt beads of sweat break out on her forehead.

She hadn't thought anything could be worse

than being trapped in this brick-lined crypt by herself. But she'd been wrong.

Sharing this dank, forbidding space with the ghost of Elyon was much, much worse.

Barely able to breathe now, Hay Lin refused to turn around and face Elyon's creepy, blank stare. She clawed at the bricks in the new wall. The rough mortar tore bloody gashes in her palms and sliced through her fingernails. But Hay Lin didn't care. She only wanted to get out. Out. Out!

"Follow me! Come with me to the other side," Elyon was saying to Hay Lin's back. "I'm your friend!"

That made Hay Lin stop sobbing, stop screaming, stop clawing. She breathed in ragged gasps. Weakly, she let her forehead rest against the brick wall.

You're not my friend, she thought. She couldn't say the words out loud because her throat was too choked with fear. But she could think them. And, silently, she shouted at the girl lurking behind her.

You're *not* Elyon, Hay Lin thought. Elyon was my friend. And a friend wouldn't have lured me into this weird, terrifying place. A friend wouldn't beg me – *force* me – to leave behind my home, my family, my world!

Again, her grandmother's face popped into Hay Lin's mind. She imagined her grandmother saying to her, "I think you'll become very good, my little Hay Lin."

A fresh round of sobs racked Hay Lin's thin body. She wanted to be good. She wanted to be strong! She wanted to fight off this new, evil version of Elyon.

That's what Grandma would have done, Hay Lin thought. For an instant, she tried to imagine her elderly, tiny grandmother as a sprightly young Guardian of the Veil. And that's when Hay Lin felt herself weakened by a stab of grief.

She collapsed to the floor – overcome with sadness. She was never going to see her sweet, loving grandmother again. She knew that. But now she wondered if she'd ever see her *parents* again! Would Elyon take her away from them forever?

Weakly, Hay Lin shook her head. She couldn't let that happen!

"No . . . " she moaned. She finally turned towards Elyon. And she found the courage –

somehow – to say her thoughts out loud: "You're not real. And this is only a nightmare."

Her words seemed only to make Elyon more determined. She shook her ghostly head slowly. Then she grinned a malevolent grin. And then the wall behind her – another looming bank of bricks and mortar – began to undulate. It was as if the stony bricks had suddenly turned to jelly.

Next, just above Elyon's blonde, shaggy head, a blue circle began forming in the bricks. It shimmered like mercury and swirled like clouds.

The glowing circle began to grow. It shivered and rumbled as it expanded into a writhing, growling . . .

Portal! Hay Lin thought desperately. That's the tunnel to Metamoor! Just like the one that erupted in the gym! I have to close it or be sucked in myself!

Before Hay Lin could even contemplate a way to close this enormous, terrifying chasm, something appeared within it.

It was a creature.

The creature was as broad as a refrigerator. Its head was covered with lumpy, rocklike protuberances, and it had bared, spiky teeth.

And its skin was bright blue.

It was Vathek – the creature who'd tried to hurt Hay Lin, Irma, and Will in the gym. Now he'd come to finish the job!

"Yes, little girl! It's all true!" the creature growled at her. His voice was choked and gurgly, as deep as a black hole. "But this time, you can't escape."

Hay Lin scrabbled backwards on the floor until she hit the wall behind her with a thud. She threw her arms over her head, preparing herself for the pain of Vathek's talons.

She imagined Elyon's treacherous hands, yanking her into the portal.

And then she pictured her grandmother's face, one last time.

"*Aaaaaagggh!*" Hay Lin screamed.

TWELVE

Will watched Cornelia stalk up to the wall that had just sprung out of the floor. She felt as though she were watching a movie she didn't quite understand. It was all happening so fast!

As Will watched Cornelia stare at the wall in determination, the facts finally sank in.

They had *definitely* found the second portal to the place Hay Lin's grandmother had told them about.

And that portal *definitely* didn't want to be found. That's why a brick wall had suddenly erupted right before their eyes, blocking them from the rest of the tunnel.

And here was the other thing Will knew.

The wall had separated them. Four of

the Guardians were in this main chamber.

Hay Lin was gone – trapped on the other side of that evil, animate wall.

And she was in extreme danger.

Who knows what else is lurking behind the wall, Will thought. Creatures of Metamoor? Some sort of vacuum cleaner that could suck Hay Lin into a new dimension?

All those unknowns filled Will with fear. But, more important, they filled her with determination! She looked from Irma to Taranee to Cornelia and felt invisible bonds stretching among them.

It's the magic bonding us together, Will said to herself. That's what I'm feeling. And that's what's going to get us out of this mess. Starting with Cornelia and her power over all earthly substances!

Will watched Cornelia plant her feet and grit her teeth. Then Cornelia pressed her hands to the dark, brooding bricks of the wall. She squeezed her eyes shut.

Will could practically see the magic coursing through Cornelia. Her slender body vibrated with power. Her arms pulsed with it. And out of her palms emanated the now familiar green rings of cosmic energy.

A hole began to form in the brick wall. It was small. And inside of it, Will could see only blackness.

It's just beginning, Will thought. She almost smiled in anticipation. Then she felt her back stiffen and her eyes squeeze shut. She was bracing herself for a shower of brick shards and shattered mortar bits. Her muscles tensed, ready to pounce through the large opening Cornelia's magic was about to drill through the wall.

Then Will heard a loud noise.

Whhuuump!

The sound was like a monster taking a huge bite out of something. Or a vacuum cleaner swallowing up something solid.

It did not sound like magic breaking effortlessly through a brick wall.

With a sinking heart, Will opened her eyes. And then she screamed in alarm.

The wall had changed all right. But the little hole that Will had seen within it hadn't widened. Instead, it extended itself into a tall tower. A sort of tentacle, made entirely of bricks, had grown out of the wall, shooting at Cornelia with the precision of a frog's tongue.

With one gulp, the tentacle swallowed up both of Cornelia's hands. The bricks swirled around her hands, binding them together as effectively as a pair of handcuffs might have done.

The tentacle grew and grew. Now it was swallowing Cornelia's wrists. Next, it moved up to her elbows! Then the tube of bricks began jerking back and forth, dragging Cornelia to and fro.

Cornelia didn't – or couldn't – scream. She merely looked over her shoulder in terror. And – with her large, frightened eyes – she begged Will for help.

"The house is alive!" Will cried to Irma and Taranee. "Let's stick together."

As the girls clung to each of her arms, Will tried to patch a plan together in her mind.

Okay, she thought desperately, we just have to–

Braaaaaaaaammm!

–get out of the way! Will thought. Another wall was barreling up through the floor!

Will jumped backwards. Then she found herself gazing in shock at an enormous tower of bricks.

This new wall was not a horizontal blockade

like the one that had trapped Hay Lin. Instead, it was a circular stack of bricks. As it grew, like Jack's bean stalk on a rampage, it plunged right between Will, Taranee, and Irma.

Will stumbled backwards.

Taranee leaped to one side.

And Irma jumped away so fast she landed on her backside, directly opposite Will.

"Holy cow!" she screamed.

Almost instantly, another wall rose up in front of Irma, completely blocking her from Will's view. From what Will could see, there'd been only a few feet between the side of their original tunnel and the new wall. Which meant Irma was now trapped in a claustrophobic cell of bricks!

Will spun around to look for Taranee. She almost sobbed with relief when she realised that she could still see her.

Quickly Will's relief turned to horror as Taranee was attacked by a brick wall. This time, the wall took the shape of a cylinder, whirling around Taranee's feet. Then, the bricks began stacking around her legs, her waist, her chest. . . .

Before Will could react, Taranee was

encased in a cylinder of bricks. It was as if she had fallen into a smokestack. Only her head poked out of the top.

Will started to run to her friend.

And that's when the walls turned on her.

A solid slab of concrete erupted only inches from her toes. It hurtled a dozen feet into the air and took Will with it! She found herself hanging from the top of the wall by her fingertips. Her feet scrabbled on the wall's smooth, slablike surface. There was no toehold.

It wasn't long before her fingers started loosening.

Will glanced down over her shoulder. Maybe the stone floor wasn't too far away. Maybe if she let go, she could escape with little more than a sprained ankle or a couple of cuts and bruises.

But when Will was able to focus on what was beneath her, she saw no floor.

It had disappeared.

She was teetering over a black, bottomless abyss!

"No!" Will cried. She pumped her legs, kicking at the wall, trying desperately to climb over it. Even as she struggled, she realised some other horrible entity could be lurking on the other side of the wall – a fate even worse than the endless abyss below her.

"N-no!" she cried.

As if that would have done any good.

This evil is too much for us, Will thought. I don't know how to fight it. Not without my friends by my side!

Will could feel her fingers, still clutching the top of the wall, loosen further.

She could feel her resolve weakening.

She wasn't going to make it!

"I'm sorry," she whispered, hoping the other girls could somehow hear her.

And then she froze.

Because, deep in the back of her mind, she could hear something answering.

Someone answering.

And that someone was Elyon!

Will stopped struggling and merely clung to the top of the wall. She pressed her cheek against one of the cold, clammy bricks.

Her breathing slowed. Her heart stopped pounding so loudly. And Will was able to focus all her magical energies on listening. Just listening.

Before she knew it, she was hearing the

thoughts of her fellow Guardians.

Will didn't know how that could have been happening, or how she knew that that was what was happening. All she knew was that – for an instant, at least – her own thoughts somehow abandoned her and she found herself floating inside the consciousness of Cornelia.

The proof came when Elyon psychically spoke to Cornelia directly – and Will heard the message as plain as day.

"Don't struggle, Cornelia," Elyon's wispy, ghostly voice said inside her mind. "Metamoor is waiting for you."

Will felt Cornelia's indignation. Her anger. And finally . . . a tiny bit of . . . intrigue.

Before Will could communicate, "Don't do it! Don't give up" to Cornelia, she felt herself being swept into Taranee's head.

"It's pointless to fight back, Taranee," Elyon whispered.

"*Aaaaah!*" Taranee screamed. Her mind was filled with a searing red terror. And a yearning for comfort. And a . . . weariness.

She's weakening, Will thought. Taranee, don't–

Will was swept into Irma's head before she

could finish the thought. She felt the claustro-phobia of Irma's little cell. She also felt Irma's despair.

"It's pointless to fight back," Elyon said again, this time addressing Irma directly. Will distinctly felt Irma's mind fill with conviction. She believed Elyon. She was sure she was doomed.

Will tried, silently, to scream out to Irma, "You can do it! Don't give in!"

Will was swept out of Irma's mind, as inex-plicably as she had entered it. She was back in her own body. And she was clinging to survival by her very fingernails.

The wall from which she was hanging began to shudder and rumble. It was trying to shake her off. Elyon and the powerful force wanted her and her friends. It would stop at nothing to steal them away.

"No!" Will screamed one final time. And as she did, a burst of physical strength surged through her. She gave her legs one mighty kick, imagining herself bounding out of a swimming pool, as lithe and powerful as a dolphin. Then, somehow, she heaved herself up to the top of the wall!

She hooked one arm, and then the other, over the top of the wall. Letting both of her elbows hang down, she balanced on her chest.

At last, she stopped flailing with her feet. She unclenched her scuffed fingers. She was safe from the abyss – for the moment.

Now she could come up with a plan.

Something made her stop plotting almost as soon as she'd begun. It was a familiar surge of heat in her right palm. She extended her fist out, away from the evil wall, and closed her eyes. She felt jets of electricity shooting up her arm, zapping her mind and body with energy.

Next, she felt power jolt through her entire being, accompanied by an exquisite stab of pain. Her mind was humming with magic.

The first time she'd had this feeling, Will had been bewildered and terrified. But now, she knew exactly what was happening. She pried her eyes open and let conscious thought reenter her mind.

"We have to fight," she told herself. "It can't end like this. Our only chance lies in the Heart of Candracar and in our powers at their very strongest!"

And then, with a combination of extreme

strength and desperate determination, she uncurled her fingers, prying her fist open. A blast of blinding pink light shot out of her hand. But Will blinked through it.

And then she grinned.

Floating just above her outstretched hand was a medallion. It was a swirling glass orb, cradled by a gleaming curlicue of shimmering metal.

It was the Heart of Candracar.

It was their salvation.

Will watched the Heart throb and thrum before her. And then, the orb began to divide. Four shimmering teardrops separated from the medallion and hovered in its orbit. The first was blue and glimmery, swirling with barely contained power.

The next teardrop was filled with orange swirls. It danced like a flickering candle flame.

Then there was a burst of green; a sudden scent of grass and earth.

And finally, a white-edged wisp of wind.

Water.

Fire.

Earth.

And air.

Will watched the teardrops – each a distillation of the Guardians' powers – soar away. The orange teardrop shot toward Taranee's tower-like prison. The watery orb whisked into Irma's dim cell. The green one connected with Cornelia as she continued to pull desperately at her trapped arms.

The wispy teardrop of air vanished from Will's view. But she hoped it was somehow penetrating Hay Lin's wall and infusing her with magic.

Finally, Will's eyes focused on her own orb – the flaring, flashing, pink Heart of Candracar. It seared her eyes and filled her heart with joy. Power. Heat.

Will felt her body convulse. Swirls of energy wrapped around her like a shawl, whisking away her clothes.

Then, with an involuntary spasm, Will curled up into a ball. One kernel of survival instinct in her subconscious helped her cling to the wall as she transformed from girl . . . to Guardian.

When Will felt delicate wings separate from her back, and felt her limbs extend to lanky leanness, she finally allowed her body to untense. She looked down at herself.

She had changed completely. She was wearing her Guardian uniform of striped leggings, purple boots, and a tiny skirt whose waistband curled and coiled around her navel.

Yes! Will thought.

She pushed off from the wall. She hovered in the air for a moment, and then she landed.

On the floor.

Somehow, her magic had restored this tunnel back to its original state.

Gazing around her wildly, Will saw Taranee suddenly burst forth from her cylindrical fortress. Her hair fluttered around her head in shimmery tendrils, and her newly pumped biceps were flexed.

"Free!" she cried.

"Strong!" Cornelia answered from the opposite side of the room. Will turned just in time to see Cornelia bat the brick tentacle off her arms like a pesky bug. The bricks flew in all directions, and she was completely freed. She strode up to Will and Taranee, unfettered and triumphant. Her blonde locks had grown longer and silkier. Beneath her body-skimming cropped top billowed a dramatically long, purple skirt.

Next, Will turned to the wall that was trapping Irma. Irma was punching her way through it effortlessly. In a few seconds, she reduced the wall to rubble. Stepping through the dust, she strode over to join her friends. She was cocking one beautiful, arched eyebrow.

"And I'm angry!" she added boldly with a curled lip.

The girls stood for a moment, blinking at one another's splendidly transformed bodies. Then they looked at Hay Lin's wall expectantly.

But nothing happened.

Uh-oh, Will thought. Something's wrong. Why isn't Hay Lin breaking out of her prison?

There was no time to search for the answer. All Will knew was, if Hay Lin hadn't broken through the wall herself, she needed their help!

Will sprang into action. She gave Taranee, Cornelia, and Irma determined glances. They had to get ready to work together.

"Everything okay?" she said.

Taranee was gazing down at her endless, muscled legs.

"It's incredible," she cried. "I'm . . . I'm different!"

Cornelia, too, was gasping with delight. Will

had forgotten that this was the first time they'd all been together in their magical forms.

Irma, of course, was an expert at it by now.

"Cool, isn't it?" she asked. She cocked one of her hips sassily. "And that's not the best part!"

"Oh?" Taranee said.

Will watched Irma curl her hands into powerful fists. Then her huge blue eyes squinted at Hay Lin's wall.

She, like Will, was ready to use their magic to crash through the wall and rescue Hay Lin – the final link in the Power of Five.

Their fellow Guardian.

Their friend.

And as the four girls lined up, Will felt those invisible, magical bonds stretching among them again.

If we work together, she told herself, there's nothing we can't fight. There's nothing we can't accomplish.

At least, that's what Will had to believe – if she was going to save the world.

FREE!

STRONG!

AND ANGRY!

EVERYTHING OKAY, GALS?

IT'S INCREDIBLE! I'M ... I'M **DIFFERENT**!

COOL, ISN'T IT? AND THAT'S NOT THE BEST PART!

EPILOGUE:
THE MARSHES OF HEATHERFIELD.

LOOK AT ALL THESE MOSQUITOES! SHOULDN'T THEY BE ON VACATION THIS TIME OF YEAR?

BZZZZz BZZZ

THE PROBLEM IS THAT THE SEASONS ARE CHANGING! MY DAD THINKS IT'S ALL BECAUSE . . .

SPLAT!

HEY!

I HAD TO DO IT! ONE LANDED RIGHT ON YOUR NECK!

DON'T START UP AGAIN, PLEASE! THE SITUATION'S ALREADY BAD ENOUGH AS IT IS!

A TOAD! COULDN'T YOU HAVE CHANGED THE GUY INTO SOMETHING BIGGER?

SORRY, I DIDN'T THINK OF THAT. THE NEXT TIME THAT SOMEONE TRIES TO KISS ME, I'LL TURN HIM INTO AN ELEPHANT! HAPPY?

HMMM, I'VE GOT A QUESTION FOR YOU. . . .

DO TOADS HAVE LONG HAIR?

WELL, I WOULDN'T SAY SO, HAY LIN!

IN THAT CASE, IT LOOKS LIKE WE'VE FOUND HIM!

YAHOO! WE DID IT! WITHOUT YOUR HELP, I WOULD NEVER HAVE FOUND HIM.

CROAK!

YOU DO THE HONOURS, IRMA! YOU GOT HIM INTO THIS, AND NOW YOU'LL HAVE TO GET HIM OUT OF IT!

GULP! ALL OF A SUDDEN, I HAVE THIS NAGGING DOUBT!

TO CHANGE HIM BACK TO HIS NORMAL SELF, I DON'T HAVE TO KISS HIM, DO I?

TO BE CONTINUED . . .